A FANTASTIC TALE OF ISLAND ADVENTURE

THE UNDERSEA WARSHIP

SHUNRO OSHIKAWA

Translated by
SHELLEY MARSHALL

CONTENTS

PREFACE

A man who appears to be a citizen of Japan is not expected to be on a ship idly floating on the waves of the Pacific Ocean when he should be enraptured only by the captivating sight of Mount Fuji.

A laurel crown of honor and glory, and a pennant of wealth and power have already left the shore and moved onto the oceans of the world.

Who wears this crown and holds this pennant of wealth and power? He is no one other than a courageous man of the seas. This courageous man of the seas should be a valiant man of the world.

* On the occasion of the auspicious day of the Emperor's Birthday

Viscounts: Admiral Itoh and Rear Admiral Kimotsuke

Count: Lieutenant Captain Yoshii

Viscounts: Lieutenant Captain Ogasa and Lieutenant Captain Uemura

* I gave a title and a preface to this trifle of a book to bring happiness and to express my sincere thanks to all.

The thorough instruction and careful proofreading by Lieutenant Captain Uemura are not only a delight to the author, but if you, the reader, gains some knowledge about the oceans from this book, you should thank the Lieutenant Captain.

Finally, I pray for the good health of Professor Iwatani Konami in far off Berlin, the capital of Germany.

Shunro Oshikawa

1

———

JAPANESE IN FOREIGN LANDS

S ix years ago, I departed from the Port of Yokohama with the goal of traveling the world. I first journeyed to America, then crossed the rough seas of the Atlantic Ocean to amuse myself in Europe. For more than twenty months, I visited well-known historic sites in England, France, and Germany. After a long journey of nearly 37,300 miles, I arrived in Italy, a country renowned since antiquity for art. I had seen my fill of many magnificent sights and was set to return to the Japan I longed for. Tonight at eleven thirty, I will board the steamship *Crescent Moon* and set sail to the east to home. Exactly four years ago, I arrived at the famous Port of Naples of this country at noon on a clear day in the middle of May, the season of sakura blossoms.

In town, I hired one of the horse-drawn carriages waiting for passengers outside the station to take me to a hotel near the coast. After arranging for a room and having lunch, I had nothing to do for more than ten hours until the ship set sail.

Travelers on long journeys understand that in a strange

land where you know no one, waiting for the departure of a train or a boat is tedious. You try standing, sleeping, looking around for something to read, a newspaper or a magazine, but find nothing. You think maybe I'll take a nap; stroll around town; lose myself in thought; gaze into various windows; or look out at the ships arriving, departing, and floating anchored on the mirror-like surface of the Port of Naples, the patterns of their decks, the flag insignia waving on their masts, and the unique styles of the rooftops of merchant houses extending to the distant seawall. This had been the experience of a man called Hamajima Takebumi.

While still in high school about twelve or thirteen years ago, Hamajima Takebumi was my friend in the same course. He was four or five years older than I and in a different grade. We weren't acquainted the whole time, but we were adept athletes who shared a taste for spur-of-the-moment adventures. Our bond was strong, and we believed that a brotherly parting would be difficult. But he soon graduated and had greater aspirations than college. Before long, he left Japan.

First, he traveled to China then on to Europe. That was six or seven years ago. An acquaintance of mine ran into him at a major exposition in Paris, the capital of France. But in my restless wanderings, I have heard little news of him. Although patchy, I've heard from friends that these days he is heavily involved in the trading business at the huge mercantile houses erected on a prosperous port in Italy.

A prosperous port in Italy and the greatest as well is the Port of Naples. Several hundred or thousand mercantile houses stand on the pier along the coast. I wondered whether Hamajima conducted business at this port? Talk like this could be likened to trying to grab onto a cloud.

Despite the improbability, I asked the hotel proprietor who was silent until I finished my question. He slapped his bald head and said, "Oh! Mr. Hamajima. I know him well. He has a thousand employees and a dozen branch offices. Isn't it that house? Go there, that way." He thrust his head out the window and gestured.

"There...that palatial three-story building. See it over there!"

In a foreign country thousands of miles away from home, I was overwhelmed to hear from the first person I met that the familiar face of a man, a dear friend, who was born near the same mountains and rivers, is here. I couldn't contain myself, and immediately changed clothes and exited the hotel.

Following the proprietor's directions, I walked west along the boulevard for men and horses, turned left at the lone cross street, and about four or five blocks down I stopped at the third building, a magnificent brick structure with *T. Hamajima* inscribed on the entrance. I passed through a room with a fine view and heard footsteps approaching and was soon face to face with Hamajima. During the decade we had not seen each other, he had grown an impressive mustache. He appeared to be the same easygoing fellow. He greeted me with "Hey, Yanagawa. This is amazing. Just amazing."

Hearing this made me ecstatic.

Despite the mustache, our simple friendship remained. We talked about many things, hunting together in the mountains and fields long ago, accidentally shooting a farmer's duck, the hard times we've had, the spring field day when we both became the champion of our respective class and fiercely competed for the winner's flag, and many other memories. I lost track of time, but eventually noticed the whirlwind of activity in this house, the different boisterous voices coming from the surrounding rooms, and the footsteps of people rushing up and down the hall.

Hamajima had always been composed and took everything in stride. Nothing surprised him. But I noticed the harried look on the face of the maid who brought us coffee. I realized that today may be a bad time amid all of this activity and quickly looked up at him and asked, "You're busy, aren't you?"

"No, no. Don't worry," he answered and sipped his coffee as he gently stroked his mustache.

"The truth is, a few people are setting off on a trip."

Before I could ask who was going and where, he said,

"Yanagawa, suppose you stayed at this port. From here, you could tour Spain, and later set out on an expedition of America."

"Ha ha ha," I responded scratching my head.

"Our enjoyable talk about old times has made me a little late. The truth is I must leave soon. Tonight at eleven thirty, I'm leaving on a ship to return to Japan."

"What? You too?" he said staring at me, "Tonight at eleven thirty on the *Crescent Moon*?"

When I answered, "Unfortunately, yes. I've given up on Spain and America," he slapped his knee and said, "Now this is strange."

As he gazed at my face, I wondered what was strange, then he continued,

"Isn't this strange? This introduction came from heaven. The truth is my wife and son are also returning to Japan tonight on the *Crescent Moon*."

"What? Your wife and son!" I shouted in surprise. Although it's no surprise that during those ten years of no contact he would find a wife and have a child, I hadn't known about them until that moment, not to mention their returning to Japan. I was stunned.

Hamajima laughed loudly, "Ha ha ha.... You didn't know a thing about my family. Forgive me."

He promptly rang a bell and the maid returned.

"Please tell my wife, we have a special guest...."

He turned to me, moved a little closer, and continued, "The truth is...the summer two years after I established this trading company, I returned to Japan. At that time, you were traveling around Siam. On my return trip, through the good offices of a go-between, the younger sister of Captain Matsushima, who is also from our province, became my wife.

"That happened about ten years ago, the child who was born a little later is already eight years old. For a long time, I, standing in the world as a businessman, would like to see my son become, if possible, a navy man capable of defending the Empire of Japan. I deeply feel that if a Japanese child is not raised in the country of Japan, his love of country will be weak. Fortunately, my wife's older brother is a worthy military man, and for some time, I have been thinking about asking him to take my son and take full control of his education, but haven't had the opportunity.

"From letters we received from Japan earlier this month, Captain Matsushima, my wife's brother who was captain of the Imperial Warship Takao, had fallen ill while awaiting orders, of course, not seriously ill. My wife wished to visit her only brother, if possible, and, after such a long absence, gaze at the moon from home. The opportunity arose, and because the child is young, the two of them are to leave on the *Crescent Moon* tonight at eleven thirty.

"Naturally, depending on the Captain's condition, they will return sooner or later. However, the child would forever stand in the world as an admirable military man of Imperial Japan and never abandon the incomparable

Mount Fuji," he concluded. Calmly looking at me, he said, "Well, if you are also departing tonight, I would appreciate your kindness in looking after them on the ship and during their stay in Japan."

I understood completely. Hamajima Takebumi seemed as cheerful as always. He dared to cut the ties of his deep love for his only child and send him home to mold him into a military man for the Empire.

Although I had not yet met his wife, the younger sister of Navy Captain Matsushima, I felt a deep admiration for her commendable behavior of soon bidding farewell with a young child on a trip crossing thousands of perilous miles to visit her brother in his sickbed.

The more I thought about it, the more this situation resembled a novel. On a whim to seek out an old friend upon arriving at this port in a land thousands of miles overseas, without any advanced plans, I was going to board the same ship at the same time as his wife and child. My fate would be entwined with theirs on a voyage lasting several months. Just as Hamajima said, this was probably a mysterious introduction by heaven. I had been absorbed in thought for a short time when the door to room quietly opened and two people entered. Needless to say, they were his wife and beloved child.

Hamajima stood to introduce them to me, "This is my wife Harue."

He turned to her and briefly described our mysterious bond given the circumstances of my trip and how we would be sailing together to Japan. Her exclamation rang with nostalgia. She was a beautiful woman who looked to be twenty-six or twenty-seven years old, her eyebrows were delicate, her mouth superb. In a glance, I thought that his wife was the most noble woman in the world with a beautiful soul like a goddess.

When the greeting ended, his wife called over the child. A timid, pale boy approached me. His name was Hideo. He was about eight years old and wearing a tidy Western-style sailor's suit. His thick hair was oddly white. His mouth had the distinguished look of his father's. His eyes were pretty, clear like his mother's. I couldn't help associating him with the cute, little hero of the novel, *Little Lord Fauntleroy*, I read last night on the train ride from Rome.

Hideo had been born in a land thousands of miles away from Japan and rarely saw any Japanese other than his parents. I thought his young heart was wistful or elated as he looked up at me with those amazing eyes and said, "Oh, Uncle, you are Japanese!"

"I'm Japanese, like you Hideo," I said and hugged him.

"Hideo, do you like Japanese people? Do you love Japan?" I cheerfully asked.

"Yup...I like Japan a lot. I want to go home to Japan. Everyday, I will raise the Hinomaru flag and fight in the streets. The...the Hinomaru is a strong flag and will win everytime."

"That's right," I said raising the face of this cute boy. When we joyfully shouted, "The Empire of Japan. *Banzai! Banzai!*" and did a little dance. Hamajima heartily laughed, Harue narrowed her eyes and said, "My, my...Hideo is so happy," and covered her smiling mouth with a crimson handkerchief.

2

———

THE DEVIL'S HOUR ON THE DAY OF THE DEVIL

Our conversation flourished. As the sun set at the end of that long day in May, I took an opportunity to leave, "Well, I'll see you tonight at the *Crescent Moon*." A flustered Hamajima said, "Please wait...wait a moment. What are you going to do after you return to the hotel? We haven't had enough time to talk today. You should leave from my home this evening."

His wife agreed completely. Given their feelings and that I have always been uninhibited, I borrowed two grooms of the house to retrieve my luggage from the hotel, and the three of us left together.

In addition to such fine treatment, at eight o'clock that evening, I was invited with everyone from the head clerks to the servants of the house to a gathering to bid farewell.

Harue was filled with great affection for the world, the most being reserved for Hideo from whom she could never part. However, her husband Hamajima kept it all in his heart because he is a hero of the East, the type who hates crying. Not one tear flowed down a single face. No, one exception caught my eye. An elderly Italian woman seated

8

in the back row of seats. She was Hideo's nanny. A long time ago, she had come a long way from the countryside to work. She was short with white hair and looked to possess great integrity. Her head was hanging down more sorrowfully than before and tears flowed as if someone were being sent to his grave.

For some reason, I was disturbed.

"Oh, Annie is crying because she still believes this journey is foolish," said Harue looking at the old woman's face.

It was almost ten o'clock when the gathering ended. The time to board the *Crescent Moon* had come. Many people were at the sea wall to see off the Hamajima family and me, their companion who arrived in the same carriage. We went to a nearby coffee shop. I thought they might have a few things to talk about, so I tactfully went out for a stroll along the shore. Suddenly, I sensed someone following me and glanced back. In an instant, a shadow ran up to me as if tumbling. I stared at it and eventually recognized Annie, the old woman who had been sitting and crying during the farewell.

"Oh, it's you," I said and stopped walking. The old woman, still crying, put both hands together, looked up at me, and said, "Sir, I have a favor to ask of you."

"You're Annie, aren't you? What is it?" I asked.

The old woman stared at me and in a raspy voice said, "Sir...You are going to Japan with my Mistress and Hideo on the *Crescent Moon* tonight. But could you please postpone your trip?" she asked fearfully. What a strange thing to ask, I thought knitting my brow. I scrutinized her. She seemed to be in deep pain, so I couldn't rebuff her.

"Yes, I am, but I can't postpone the trip," I gently replied.

When I kindly asked, "But why are you grieving so?"

She raised her head slightly and said, "Sir, the truth is I am not that sad. I was surprised when I first heard that the Mistress and Hideo were returning to Japan, but it couldn't be helped. Only later when I heard that they were leaving tonight at eleven thirty...."

Her lips quivered as she spoke, "By leaving tonight at eleven thirty..."

"What about the ship leaving tonight?" I asked fixing my gaze on her.

Annie tapped her chest and said, "I prayed to God. You don't know this, but something is terribly wrong. Time and again I begged the Master and Mistress to postpone the departure tonight, but they just laughed and said, 'Oh Annie, you worry too much,' and wouldn't listen anymore. But Sir, I know that the Mistress and Hideo will not be safe if they leave tonight on the *Crescent Moon*."

"They won't be safe...," I interjected.

"That's right. They won't be safe," appealed a sober Annie.

"I believe you. I won't laugh at you," I pledged.

"According to legends from long ago as told by the Saint of Mt. Urbino, certain dates must not be chosen for ships to set out on journeys. People who travel on unlucky days will meet certain misfortune. This is the truth. In fact, seven or eight years ago, I begged my son not to leave. He left the house on a cursed day in October and, in the end, was captured by a frightening sea serpent. I know that if the Mistress and Hideo leave tonight, they won't be safe because today is May 16, the Day of the Devil. Tonight at eleven thirty is especially frightening. It's the Devil's Hour."

I let out a sigh as I listened, but she didn't calm down.

"Sir, don't laugh. The Devil's Hour on the Day of the Devil is the most unlucky time of the entire year. With so many other days, to leave on this day and at this time invites misfortune. And all that gold and pearls gathered on the *Crescent Moon*, which I heard about from a friendly sailor, on the rough waves of the sea is a terrifying curse. Bad luck upon bad luck. Sir, if you had an ounce of sympathy with my heart, I thought you would somehow find a way to help my Mistress and Hideo. Please postpone your departure," she said bowing and clasping her hands together.

Hearing this, I thought what nonsense! There are people in the West with tales of omens! But someone like this old woman is an oddity. Bursting out in laughter crossed my mind, but even if this were mere superstition, I carefully considered the Master's situation. I felt that a serious person should not be ridiculed flat out. I forced down the laughter that was welling up.

"Annie!" I shouted.

"Annie! I understand what you are saying. Your Master and Mistress should be congratulated for this devotion. But...," I said looking straight at her, "but what you are saying is from a bygone era. Now, the Day of the Devil is no longer a cursed day."

"Oh, Sir, are you going to make fun of me, too?" asked an expressionless Annie with her eyes closed.

"No, I will not, but there is nothing to worry about. I will protect the lives of your Mistress and Hideo," I said, but Annie's face was a mask of despair.

"Oh...this is useless," she said while crying and abruptly stood.

"Please God and Guardian Angel, please save the souls of the Mistress and Hideo," she cried and ran away as if she were a lunatic. At that moment, I could hear Hama-jima calling me to check the preparations for boarding at the service area.

3

A MYSTERIOUS SHIP

At half past ten, Harue, Hideo, and I took leave of the many people who had come to see us off and boarded a small steamship at the seawall to take us to the *Crescent Moon* anchored far off shore. Hamajima Takebumi and three companions accompanied us to the steamship.

The *Crescent Moon* was a special ship manufactured by the Eastern Shipping Company of Italy with a tonnage of 6,400 tons. It was a huge ship with four masts and two funnels. The heavy load of large quantities of iron and quite a lot of precious cargo, like gold and pearls, for a voyage headed to many ports in China and Japan made the draft of the ship so deep, it appeared to be sinking.

When we reached the gangway of the *Crescent Moon*, the crewmen knew we would be boarding from the passenger list and came running and efficiently transferred our luggage. The greeter doffed his hat, and respectfully made a path through the throng of people on deck to guide us to the first-class cabin near the center of the ship. On any steamship, the center cabin is the most desired spot, even among the first-class cabins. You may wonder why. That is where the rocking of a ship at sea is felt the least. Many competitors vied for this room, Germans with bristly mustaches, and Frenchmen with aquiline noses. Fortunately, due to the exceptional hard work of the renowned and prosperous Hamajima Takebumi, "a famous and wealthy Japanese man" living in Naples, we occupied the best cabins. All was fine because Harue and Hideo's cabin was adjacent to mine.

As a lone traveler, I could blithely toss my bag into my cabin and visit Harue's cabin. Hideo was sitting on her lap, and she was conversing with the boy and the three other people. She noticed me and said, "Oh, you've already settled in." Her graceful frame hurriedly stood to welcome me.

"What? Yanagawa doesn't have luggage to arrange," roared Hamajima, "Well," he said offering me a chair and I joined the group. The time to leave soon arrived. During the course of the assorted conversations, we heard the clanging of a bell echoing throughout the ship.

"Hey...what's that sound?" asked Hideo looking at his mother with widened eyes. Harue looked at him, but said nothing. Hamajima Takebumi quietly stood, glanced at his three companions, and said, "Well, the time has come for us to go."

By the Law of the Sea, ten to fifteen minutes before a ship leaves port, a bell is heard echoing throughout the ship, and all those not taking the journey must disembark. When the time to leave came, after Hamajima shook my hand and said some warm parting words to me and a few more words to his wife, he drew his beloved child close to hug him. As he patted the boy's thick hair, he said, "Hideo, you and I will be apart for a long time. As I have often said, you must not forget that my wish is for you to become a great man of the world, a capable naval officer, and a defender of the Empire of Japan." He smiled at the boy who was nodding and prompted his three companions to leave the cabin.

We, who had been seen off earlier, were now seeing others off from the ship. I led Hideo by the hand and helped a sad Harue out onto the deck. On this evening of the thirteenth day, not even a wisp of a cloud was in the midnight blue sky. The moon was bright. Three or four warships of some country were anchored near the far off shore and continuously illuminated the surface of the sea with search lights so bright it resembled daylight. The buoys bouncing in the light between the waves reminded one of soldiers.

When Hamajima reached the gangway of the ship, he turned to look at the faces of his wife and child, then he looked at me as if something weighed heavy on his heart.

"Yanagawa, although I've said this before, please take care of Harue and Hideo...."

The extent of his anxiety was uncharacteristic given his usual impressive demeanor, and he increasingly seemed unable to leave as if he had been captured by some strong force in the air.

I later thought that perhaps this was a premonition, but, at that time, I felt he was merely apprehensive about the separation. I nodded and smiling replied, "Hamajima, I swear on my life to protect the lives of your wife and child," and shook hands with each of his three companions as they descended the gangway onto the small steamship. Immediately, the small steamship kicked up waves and returned to the seawall. Two or three agitated sea birds cried as in a dream. Amid the heartrending scene of the passengers, Hideo innocently said, "Papa left by himself. Is he going home already?" he said clinging to his mother's delicate hand. This noble woman's heart filled with compassion. Moonlight as bright as daylight surrounded the husband she had sadly seen off. The form of the small steamship gradually faded away until only a long trail of smoke lingered.

"Harue, shall we go up to the deck and have a look around?" I suggested. I felt that looking at a bustling scene when one is melancholy diverts the heart somewhat. I led them to the bow that appeared full of life at that moment.

The time to leave port came quickly, and the area was crowded. Officers dressed in light clothing were dashing about. Many sturdy crewmen formed lines at their posts and raised the stern gangway. Under the orders of the first mate now on the bow deck, a group of able-bodied seaman hurried to the winder and readied to raise the anchor cable on the next command. The portly barrel-chested ship's captain on the bridge stroked his red beard as he proudly and contemptuously surveyed the scene. I stood among the groups of two and three passengers and looked around at this eye-popping scene that included a Belgium with a strikingly pale complexion, a young French gentleman with a mustache painted on like a sword with cosmetics, a German military officer with a nose reddened by too much drink, an Italian actress who epitomized a beautiful woman, and a wealthy Indian with a very black complexion. I was chatting with Harue, when out of nowhere, a sailor behind me cried out, "Hey...hey! Whoa! Watch out!" At that instant, I heard something crash onto the deck.

When I quickly turned to look, two or three sailors had been using a pulley to raise a light high on the fore-mast. It was the masthead light for signifying safe progress during a voyage. The connection snapped for some reason, and the bulb fell from a mast just twenty feet high. In an instant, the bulb crashed into the bridge where the Captain was standing and smashed into pieces. The lamplight went out, and the startled Captain lost his footing trying to dodge the glass and fell back two or three steps off the bridge. The sailors flushed from surprise. The agitated Captain stood up. He looked outraged, but he couldn't be angry at himself. He slapped his barrel-shaped belly and scowled fiercely at the sailors. A noble, balding English gentleman with a long beard was standing near me. He was trembling from the sight of that dramatic scene and cried out, "Oh my! This is bad...very bad luck. Heaven help us! This ship may be cursed."

What?! Superstition again! What is going on today?

Of course, there may not be a profound reason. It must be chance. Nonetheless, it seemed strange. Anyone would feel that way. If a minor but strange event occurs when setting out to battle or on a journey, you can't help but feel a bit concerned. In particular, the goal of our *Crescent Moon* is to cross thousands of miles. On the way, the ship will pass through treacherous waters like the famous Mediterranean Sea, the Red Sea, and the Indian Ocean, but the white masthead light that should signal the safe voyage of the steamship had been smashed to pieces; its light extinguished; and simultaneously, the Captain, the leader of this ship, had fallen off the bridge and appeared disgusted and angry. Are these omens that the *Crescent Moon* may be cursed? These events definitely didn't put you at ease.

Naturally, fantastic ideas like these are easily dismissed, but I felt uneasy as I recalled Annie's talk earlier about the Devil's Hour on the Day of the Devil and Hamajima's uncharacteristic concern. When I considered leaving this place and glanced at Harue, she also seemed to be troubled by the situation and the mutterings of the old English gentleman.

"Why don't we go to the stern?" I urged and took a few steps in that direction.

When we reached the stern of the ship and looked around, there were a few people. The bright moon reflected off the scrubbed deck with a misty film.

"Just as I thought, it's quiet here," said Harue managing a sad smile. She walked over to the side with Hideo and looked at the far-off pier while leaning against the railing.

"Hideo, do you remember that tall mountain over there?" she asked and pointed at a towering mountain southeast of Naples, their home for so long.

"It looks like Mount Molise. See I remembered," replied Hideo looking at his mother.

"Well then, what is that place where all those electric lights are shining, that place where those five or six chimneys are lined up?"

"Via San Gallo. Mama, that's where are our house is," said Hideo resting both of his hands on the railing.

"Papa's probably home already."

"Yes, he's home. Right now, he's probably telling Nanny and the head clerk Mr. Smith how bravely you boarded the ship," Harue attentively told her son as she pressed her cheek, which seemed like a jewel, against his thick hair. This may be Harue's only comfort. I thought it insensitive to intrude on this scene, so instead of going toward them, I moved away slightly and lay down on a deck chair.

I took in the scenery, the moonlight this evening flooded the wide Bay of Naples with light. I could see the rotating beacon appear then disappear on the barely visible Ischia Island. I have no words to describe the white snow remaining on the peak of Mount Molise rising high in the sky and reflected by the glistening moonlight.

The scene was a dreamscape. On the gold-tipped waves running from the far-off pier brightly lit by electric lights to the ship, several hundred floating warships, departing ships, and arriving ships obeyed the Law of the Sea with a white light on the foremast, a green light on the starboard side, and a red light on the port side. The anchored ships resembled giant birds sleeping on the sea. I had never seen such a breathtaking sight. Fascinated, I could not look away and memorized the evening.

As I looked all around, something caught my eye. Anchored about five hundred meters away was a steamship. The searchlights of this warship of some country brightly lit up the area. I could see equipment on the deck and felt as though I could grab it. The tonnage of that ship was 1,000 gross tons. Its hull was painted black. There were two masts on two funnels. I could see that it wasn't a warship. I couldn't tell whether it was a merchant vessel, a mail boat, or a ship with some other special purpose. Although its appearance was not suspicious, I do recall being struck by something peculiar. Its draft appeared to be unusually deep. One thousand gross tons is a very solid structure, but several pallets of guns may have been loaded below deck. The black smoke belching from the two funnels probably meant it was preparing to leave port. In an instant, the anchor at the bow was raised and the ship began to advance.

I casually searched my pockets for binoculars and focused them to inspect that deck. At that same moment on the other ship, a man who seemed to be a sailor was intently looking through binoculars at my ship. That was odd. When my line of sight unexpectedly collided with his, he instantly flung his binoculars away and turned away pretending not to have seen me. I cocked my head upon seeing that rather strange behavior.

For some unknown reason, a certain story sprang to mind at that moment. It was an unforgettable incident that occurred last fall during my journey from America to Europe. I had struck up a friendship with an old English sailor. Of the many interesting tales told by that old sailor, the one that stayed with me was a story about the most frightening sea route in the world, the Indian Ocean. Far off the island of Madagascar in eastern Africa is a pirate's island that is unknown even in the dreams of men.

Naturally, this isolated island cannot be found on any map of the world. Several hundred pirates who have deceived fierce gods formed a brigand. Seven fast and sturdy pirate ships continuously roam the sea lanes in that region. Sometimes, the ships set sail to coasts on the far-off Atlantic Ocean. When they encounter a ship loaded with precious cargo, they attack and sink it. They rage with despicable greed. Even some of his fellow European and American sailors were unaware of this fact. Unfortunately, the shrewd actions of this pirate brigand die in words, like incoming and retreating winds.

These pirates don't know how to track down their quarry. Instead they always target ships loaded with first-rate precious cargo. Because ships like that are seldom seen, the pirates have conspired for some time with tyrannical nations in Europe for profit. Bribery amounting to nearly fifty million dollars is delivered annually in return for covert protection. Sometimes, a ship will anchor in a trading port as a ship with legal registration, fly the merchant flag of that powerful country above its deck, and behave audaciously. This is truly scandalous.

By some baffling actions of my nerves, this tale suddenly came to mind as I looked at this mysterious ship with two funnels and two masts. If the old sailor's words are true, could that be one of these ships? As I pondered this grim affair of pirate ships, the mysterious ship gradually accelerated. As she stealthily passed on the port side of the *Crescent Moon*, I made out the name emblazoned on her stern glinting in the light radiating from my ship's lamp, *Sea Snake*. As I looked, the waves were kicked up, and the ship vanished into the vast darkness.

I wondered aloud, "Why have these mysterious events occurred one after the other today?"

"Is something wrong?" startled, both Harue and Hideo turned.

"Harue," I started to speak, but caught myself. What if this talk were nothing more than my imagination. I considered whether I would trouble the kind heart of this beautiful person if I spoke carelessly.

"No. It's nothing," I said laughing loudly. At exactly this moment, seven bells rang out on deck to announce eleven thirty. Simultaneously, a whistle resembling the roar of a lion sounded to signal our leaving the port. At last, the *Crescent Moon* entrusted with our fates slowly pressed forward.

4

A SCRAP OF NEWSPAPER

I **lingered on the** side of the deck opposite Harue and
Hideo and admired the scene until we left the mouth
of the bay. I recall the fading lights of the Bay of Naples
and the piercing, chilly evening winds before we left the
deck. We said goodnight, and Harue and Hideo returned
to their cabin and I to mine. In my cabin, I could clearly
hear eight tolls of the bell on deck.

"Ah! It's already midnight!" I said to myself. It was
quite late. The waves were gentle that evening and the ship
swayed very little. Many of the passengers were probably
peacefully dreaming. The only sounds were the noise from
the steam engine and occasional stomping footsteps of the
crewmen on duty going back and forth on the deck.

I changed into my bedclothes and lay across my bed.
For some reason, however, I wasn't the least bit tired. A
bright light radiated from the lamp hanging in the center
of the room. The air weighed heavily on my head, as if an
evil spirit lurked nearby, and I found sleeping difficult. You
too may have had this experience, but this time I couldn't

sleep at all. As I became more aggravated, even wilder thoughts raced through my head and kept me awake.

I decided to get up. I wanted a cigar, but didn't want to bother going to the smoking room. Although this was a minor infraction of the ship's regulations, I decided to smoke in my cabin. I searched my suitcase, but couldn't find even one. I suddenly remembered the many gifts Hamajima had given me at our departure from the Port of Naples. One was a square package wrapped in newspaper that I thought might be a pack of cigarettes. I quickly opened it and found the finest cigars! Hurray! I lit one. While looking around as I puffed away, I noticed the newspaper wrapping.

"Ah! This is a Japanese newspaper," I snatched it up automatically.

As a globetrotter who left Japan two years ago, I sometimes heard about unusual events from home at Japanese diplomatic and consular offices, but rarely read anything like a Japanese newspaper, so I was swept away with nostalgia. I quickly smoothed out the wrinkles and saw that this was a Tokyo newspaper from about eighteen months ago. A year and a half ago, I was still on the American continent. Although the newspaper was old, that didn't matter. I was filled with nostalgia and determined to read every word. My eyes instantly went to an article in the first column. It was general news printed on the left side of the second page.

Where is Reserve Navy Captain Sakuragi?

As the reader knows, a powerful explosive was discovered a few years ago and was effective in improving two or three weapons, like buoy mines and explosive rings. Since returning last year from a pleasure trip in England, Reserve Navy Captain Sakuragi Shigeo, a man well known in military circles, has been deeply involved in strategy and in making an astounding military discovery that will contribute to the defense of our nation.

Although you have heard an inkling about the reasons for this dire scheme, perhaps, the time has come to divulge it, or some other consideration has come into play. At the beginning of this month, a large sailing ship named the Bay of Waves was purchased from a certain merchant ship company in Yokohama and secretly loaded with food, coal, volatile oils, wax coils, wire rope, various chemicals, and many materials impossible for the general public to imagine. But it disappeared unnoticed by us.

When the figure of Captain Sakuragi disappeared and the sailing ship was no longer anchored in the port, thirty-seven sailors who had served under his command for many years and obeyed him like a god or a parent also vanished. The Captain with his crew seem to have slipped out under the cover of darkness.

This incident was top secret even within the naval service. No one knows their whereabouts. One possible clue came from an English mail boat that arrived last night at the Port of Yokohama. In the dead of night four or five days ago, they had a confirmed sighting of a large sailing ship flying the Japanese flag near North Borneo Island.

If the profile of that ship fits that of the Captain's sailing ship, the suspicion is that he may be taking a sea route past the China Sea and not toward the Indian Ocean.

From the beginning, he kept his plan top secret, classified, and impossible to guess. In any event, if he possesses an extraordinary intellect and a grand objective, he may bring about some unforeseen achievement from some unexpected direction. We do not know and again eagerly await what will be revealed.

Any one, no matter how disinterested, who read this article would be deeply moved, but I was particularly moved. Several years ago, before I set out on my travels, I met Navy Captain Sakuragi. I was on a trip to Hokkaido I had planned to take that summer. While on a steamship from Yokohama to Hakodate, I happened to meet the Captain. He was about thirty-two or thirty-three years old. He had a commanding but pleasant personality, a sparkle in his eyes, and a deep, booming voice. I believed him to be a capable and bold man. This man had become a topic in the newspapers and was resolved to take a journey called into question by the world. What is his destination? What is his objective? Considering the great military invention, the large sailing ship, thirty-seven sailors, and the chemicals all together, although nebulous, anything imaginable was possible.

Today, many countries throughout the world are training soldiers, polishing their weapons, and expending all their energy, particularly on naval power. England, France, Russia, and Germany are fighting for power over us. However, current power disputes are often centered in lands in the East. These constant violations burden China and Korea.

These days, the Empire of Japan, as a rising nation in the East, bears a heavy burden and requires extraordinary determination and true ability to maintain peace in the East and at least preserve the dignity of our nation. However, the resources of our nation are limited, as is any increase in warships. Gentlemen who mull over the state of the nation are concerned and are always adopting measures to address these issues.

Captain Sakuragi is essentially a man who laments the state of the nation. When our conversation touched on this point on the ship to Hokkaido, he reached into his pocket and showed me a portion of a mysterious new-style poem he had written yesterday evening as relief from the tedium of the inn. Aren't the refined tastes of the intrepid warrior interesting?

This is that poem.

> Over the Indian Ocean, a high
> moon, sleeping winds.
> Above the mirrored surface of
> the sea
> Mist suddenly rises.
> A whale bellows.
> A dragon leaps.
> Look! Giant waves rage, the sky
> splits.
> Black clouds hover low over the
> ocean.
> A flash. Electricity?
> A roar. Thunder?
> Artillery fire. Booming rolling
> thunder.
> Look! Escape into the smoke.
> The moon illuminates a face of
> shame.
> Several hundred cut through the
> waves.
> Flags of ancient warships coil and
> release.

The whale flees, the flying dragon
    pursues!
The courageous dragon, the brave
    whale.
Black smoke without despair. Blow-
    ing. Shadows hide.
This whale, a strange land.
Until the border of the dominion is
    reached.
A surge hits. A place with treasure.
A mountain of waves becomes a
    ship.
A thousand winds become the sail.
Rampant domination lost. This
    alliance of European fleets.
What is the strategy? In the East.
    The rising sun seizes a key
    position.
A light shining on the sea. This
    name is the exalted Japanese
    fleet
Japan is the East. The small nation,
    like the flying dragon.
Europe, brave like the whale. Braver
    than an alligator.
The world scowls. A great nation.
Doubt.
The big defeated, the small victori-
    ous. Why?
Listen to the defeated general.
He climbs up to the bridge. He looks
    up and laments the stars.
A million huge warships. Swarms of
    officers and men.

Guns. Swords. Gunpowder.
What does the Japanese naval fleet
    fear?
Like the leaves of trees scattering in
    autumn.
Forced into wreckage on the sea.
Advance, fleets of England, France,
    German, and Russia.
By chance. Japan has a mysterious
    charm.
This. The Gatling gun? No.
The Ciel Bleu torpedo boat? No.
A huge weapon.
Still unseen.
Still unheard.
Comes like the wind. Leaves like the
    wind.
Like a pod of killer whales in
    pursuit.
Like being struck by electricity.
Look, our fleet demolished. The
    great magical power of
    lightning.
Ah, you should be afraid. Very
    afraid.
The dragon tears apart the Sea of
    Japan.
Black clouds fly above the East.
Light from the sun pierces the sky.
A huge weapon hidden by the sea.

This bizarre poem was, perhaps, a tax collected from the new school of masters. On the deck of the steamship belching a clear wind under the moonlight, a shout of joy escaped me during the recitation in that sonorous voice as the hilt of the Captain's sword swung behind him. Of course, I thought of nothing in particular at that time, but now is the first time I recalled that occasion.

In any case, according to the old newspaper article, Captain Sakuragi had planned this secret journey over a year and a half ago. As I said earlier, I was still touring America, perpetually wandering from place to place. The information in the article was new to me. What will the Captain do next? He may eventually achieve his objective and return to Japan. Given Captain Sakuragi's disposition, without a doubt, much hope can be found in his actions. Because he will not stop until the plan achieves his objective, when the Captain reappears in this world, an immense achievement will no doubt have been realized. Therefore, if Captain Sakuragi returns to Japan, his exploits will shine brighter than the sun and the moon.

As I wandered from place to place, some rumors never reached my ears. I've visited Japanese diplomatic and consular offices in various countries and never heard a whisper of this. This proves to me that the Captain concealed his whereabouts, which are still unknown to the world. Still many guesses bubbled up in my mind when I wondered, "Where is the Captain?"

At that moment, the bell tolled twice. (Signal bells onboard a ship cycle from one to eight strikes every four hours.)

"Ah, it's one o'clock." I yawned. I could ruminate over this forever. However, I had to be prudent about the effects of staying up this late on my health. I rolled up the old newspaper that became the source of my imaginings and pushed it into a corner of the cabin, and forced myself to lie down.

At first, my head felt queer. I struggled to erase many

fantastic ideas, but like before, more floated up. I was haunted by the visions swimming in my head: the Devil's Hour on the Day of the Devil, Annie's face, the shattered white masthead light, the mysterious ship, and the binoculars. From the fatigue of the daytime hours, I fell into scattered dreams before the signal bell struck two o'clock.

5
———

PIANO AND BOXING

The following morning at half past eight, I was abruptly awakened by the sound of bells. The morning sun over the sea shined through the porthole illuminating the cabin. On a ship, the eight-thirty bell usually announced breakfast.

"Oh no! I've overslept." I bounded out of bed, dressed, combed my hair, and rushed to the dining room. When I arrived, the barrel-chested captain was solemnly seated at the head of a splendid table, as is the rule on a ship. The first-class passengers from England, France, Germany, Russia, Belgium, and Italy all elegantly dressed were seated on both sides. Mixed in that group, I saw the beautiful Harue and the cute Hideo. The boy quickly stood when he saw me. He looked like he had missed me. He said, "Good morning," and cutely bowed. I returned the greeting, "Good morning," as I walked over to him. I noticed that Harue seemed lonely.

When I asked, "Did you sleep well last night, Harue?" a slight smile appeared on her face.

"No, I have not acclimated to the ship, but he slept well," she answered.

Her words did not surprise me. The pale blue tinge near her white cheeks was evidence of a lack of sleep. Breakfast on the ship was a light meal of cold meat and soup, rice curry, coffee, pretty fruit-filled pastries, and pineapple. When we finished, Hideo headed to the deck, and his mother and I had no choice but to follow.

Looking out from the deck, I saw that the *Crescent Moon* had passed the coast of the Island of Capri last night. I looked up and saw the Lycosia cliffs as we sailed by. It was the middle of May, not too hot and not too cold. This beautiful scene was like a picture. The sun was already high above the horizon and its brilliant light fell on the water. The silhouettes of tiny white sails reflected off the surface of the vast sea. Flocks of seagulls serenely flew by. Naturally, both my heart and my mind were refreshed, and I forgot about the unpleasant events of the previous evening.

Harue's complexion brightened, and she gently exhaled. She gazed intently at the sea, not even brushing aside the stray hairs blown into her face by the south winds. Hideo couldn't contain his delight. He frolicked like a baby lamb in a meadow. From time to time he ran up to me with a question about some rigging on the deck, or went to his mother to hold her hand and point at some far off island.

"Look! That's Erino Island we can see from the third floor of our house in Naples. It looks like an old bald man fishing."

They seemed content.

The sun was high in the sky, and the winds were cool as the ship sailed straight as an arrow. I sat on a deck chair and pondered my situation. Until last night, I had journeyed several thousand miles. In all that time, there had never been even one person to talk with during happy or sad times.

In the morning, I welcomed the invigorating light of the morning star. In the evening, I gazed alone at the magnificent sunsets. But yesterday, by chance, I met a countryman in a land far away from home. By some strange coincidence, like an act of heaven, I am fortunate to be returning home on the same ship as the beautiful Harue and the adorable Hideo.

The *Crescent Moon* carried nearly five hundred passengers, and with the crew, over seven hundred people. Of these, we three were the only Japanese. We were tied to each other by some mysterious bond and had all entrusted our fates to this ship for several thousands of miles on the sea. If divine protection exists, as we passed over the Indian Ocean and the China Sea, I fervently prayed for nothing more than the waves to be serene like today, for us to continue to celebrate the calm journey, and to soon be able to look down at the tops of the cotton roses.

Several thousand miles from the Port of Naples, we passed an archipelago and entered the Mediterranean Sea. Our coal and drinking water were replenished at Port Set. We sailed past the Isthmus of Suez guided by the currents. Since ancient times, navigators have lost courage at the world's most treacherous spot and rode on surges like rough seas of blood called a dead sea also known as the Red Sea. By inexplicable actions of the atmosphere above the sea seen from the starboard and port sides, a distant island seems to be close, while a nearby ship appears to be far away.

Consequently, an unknown number of unexpected calamities have occurred. The ships shipwrecked by this ocean have already sunk to the bottom of the sea. Within the spectacular backdrop of the remains of mastheads appearing and disappearing in the waves, the ship advanced and eventually reached the Gulf of Aden, which could be dubbed the harbor of the Indian Ocean.

The skies were clear and the seas calm everyday of the two-week-long sea route until we saw the island of Socotra far off in the vast blue sea mist. The sailors who pass through life on a cushion of waves said this had been an unprecedented good voyage. Nothing out of the ordinary had occurred during that time. Only two or three memories suggest that a god of misfortune was hidden somewhere on this ship during that peaceful time.

When the ship left the Strait of Messina, one passenger jumped into the sea to bring about his cruel end. One Chinese passenger in steerage fell seriously ill while we were still in Italy's territorial waters and died somewhere between the islands of Candia and Cerigo. Following the Law of the Sea, many crewman including the Captain gathered on deck. An English missionary gave the eulogy, then the remains were buried at sea. Although these events were wretched, there were also a few amusing ones.

On a long voyage to any destination, diversions on the ship include entertainment like farces, dramatic plays, and dances. The preparations are superb, especially, for the longest voyage in the entire world between Europe and the East. The *Crescent Moon* provided these entertainments, which we often attended. This evening, there would be a rare recital in the ballroom fitted with dazzling electric lights. Consequently, several hundred Europeans and Americans, young and old, gathered with an excitement bordering on madness.

One elderly, bald French gentleman appeared to have been quite skilled in the old days. The scene was rather comical. He picked up a violin as if he were about to play, but suddenly seemed to forget the score and played nothing as he stroked his head. Generally, Europeans and Americans are good at memorization. Both study particular works and are pleased with themselves. When Harue and I took our seats, a prim matronly German lady was playing the piano.

She seemed to be rather arrogant and haughtily peered down at the faces of the audience from the piano stage throughout the performance. Although I didn't see any virtuosity in the singing by a voice that often sounded like a goose, the singer was quite smug. And when the performance ended, she had an air of triumph, flared her skirt like a peacock, and returned to her seat.

I wondered what sort of person would take the stage next. As I chatted with Harue, I gazed at the chair. No one came out after a short time. Perhaps, that person was taken aback by the woman with the goose voice. As I wondered, an Englishman made a beeline to us and in a loud voice said, "Well, it's your turn. As representatives of Japan, what will you do?" The entire audience applauded.

"What? Who me?" I hesitated. Unfortunately, the eyes of the many members of the white race fell on us, members of a different race. Because I am essentially an unrefined man, I remained silent in the face of this surprise attack. Harue also demurred, but this man did not back down from his request. Moreover, several hundred people were clapping. I could hear derisive laughter coming from the chair beside me. It was the lady with the goose voice. She whispered to a young man seated nearby loud enough for us to hear, "No matter what you say, you're wasting your time. We have never seen a koto nor a shamisen nor held a crude instrument. Why should a Japanese person sing some highbrow Western song?"

"What a rude woman," I thought as I bit my lip. But

sadly, I'm a thoroughly unaccomplished entertainer. If only I knew something about these things, but it's too late to regret not having learned the verse of some popular London song. When I looked at Harue's face, she seemed to have overheard the slight and had become a bit flustered. Her willow-like eyebrows gently moved and furtively look at me in what seemed to be a sign of confidence in her ability. When I nodded in silence, she quietly stood. As she stepped onto the piano stage, she said "Hopefully, at least, I won't sully your ears...." Immediately, echoes resembling jewels tumbling on the sound board made one suspect that God dwelled in the piano.

The verse recited with an elegant melody was, "The Young Girl in Chrysanthemum Country," a very popular tune at that time in society circles in Paris. It told the story of a beautiful young Japanese woman dressed as a dancer wandering on the surface of the Seine River on a moonlit night. Each verse of this elegant and clever piece was brilliant and amusing. A sweet voice resembling celestial nymphs dancing in the sky fluttered like flowers or leaves onto the heartless stage. A hush fell over the room. When the song ended, the room erupted in applause. Both ladies and gentlemen rushed to the sides of the stage and surrounded Harue, as she carefully descended, to shake her hand and to shower praise on her exceptional musical skill.

The woman with the goose voice was agape. She was flushed red and her eyes bulged, probably regretting her earlier imprudent words. The echoes of the piano that evening still linger in my ears and counted as one of the most stirring moments of the evening.

There have been many other interesting events. Two days after the recital, the ship was passing the shores of an archipelago. Many of the passengers had gathered on deck and were absorbed in various games when someone suggested a footrace.

Today, the world's largest ship is two hundred and thirty yards long, more than two city blocks. On this ship, a race of four round trips on the deck from bow to stern covered about three hundred yards. The champion would receive a beautiful gift from the Ladies' Auxiliary of the crew.

Many fit men from England, France, Germany, as well as, Italy, Switzerland, and Russia patted their legs and kicked out in preparation. I was also drawn into the race, and we dashed off at the report of a gun. Unfortunately, the first to cross the finish line was a blazingly fast French reserve naval officer. Second place went to a naval officer attaché to the Italian embassy. I squeaked into third place. It wasn't very interesting, but this time, the ability of a Japanese man had been seen. When sumo was subtly suggested, a mob instantly gathered.

The leader of the mob that rushed over to me was a German legal scholar who possessed tremendous physical strength. Although he knew a little about judo, I won with a flawless *haraigoshi* throw. I also threw the next four comers. But a fifth man, a Russian military officer, lumbered over. He stood nearly six feet tall and was savage like the King of the Asuras. He grabbed both my arms with all his might and vigorously spun me around once. I was caught off guard. But wait! I held my ground and struggled desperately for a short time, and little by little I managed to get down on one knee.

Word of this struggle rapidly spread throughout the ship. Admirable elderly people and teeth-grinding young people created a commotion. I even won strange praise like "The Japanese man is a type of iron. If you asked why, it's because it is black and sturdy." I felt proud for a moment, but a major incident occurred. This is what I want to tell you about. I heard a rumor that a man, a master American boxer, happened to be traveling on this ship. I was not familiar with this master. I heard the proposal of "If the Japanese is that strong, wouldn't a boxing match be great?"

I had seen boxing matches, but had never been in one. However, in the face of a proposal like this, a man's pride makes him fight to see what will happen. My unfamiliarity with boxing couldn't be helped. However, after consider-able pain, I lost consciousness and toppled to the deck. My pride was cruelly shattered.

Harue was quite worried and admonished me as dew clouded her bright eyes. "You must not treat your body so poorly." I was actually disappointed, but resigned. For the time being, thanks to the boxing, there would be no offer for a serious contest, which angered me.

The day after the fight, another upheaval arose. As we headed to Hong Kong for entertainment, the tiger of a circus stunt rider traveling on this ship escaped its cage. Pandemonium filled the ship. There were angry sailors, screaming Chinese, and fainting ladies. Upon seeing the masthead light smashed to pieces as the *Crescent Moon* was leaving the port, an elderly Englishman had murmured, "Heaven help us! This ship may be cursed." As he fled the deck for his cabin, he slid headfirst down the hatch and couldn't get up. He may have accidentally cursed himself. Eventually, the tiger was captured, but not before seven or eight people had been injured.

Throughout this medley of incidents, as expected, Hideo had been playing energetically on the deck, running and jumping all around, and had befriended a jocular old Englishman with the unusual name of Rip.

Everyday they would laugh and play. However, once in a while, they got into trouble. One day, the old man made a diamond-shaped kite to fly on the deck. Just as the sinister-looking captain was on the bridge unfairly reprimanding some sailors, the kite string caught his hat and sent it flying. The very particular, fussy captain flushed beet red and turned toward us. He glared at the angelic Hideo for a long time, but was unable to get mad. He turned his barrel-chested hulk as he grumbled and set off after his hat.

Although a variety of unusual events occurred, they're fairly tedious, so I won't bore you with them. With this backdrop, the *Crescent Moon* entrusted with our fate left the Gulf of Aden and entered the rough seas of the Indian Ocean.

6

———

FIERY EXPLOSIONS

By dusk on the fifth day after entering the high, rough waves of the Indian Ocean, time had passed without incident. On the evening of the sixth day, as was my custom after dinner, I went to the common room above the dining hall. There I met Harue and told Hideo tales of the adventures of the explorer Captain Cook, the heroic exploits of the tiger-hunting samurai Kato Kiyomasa, or the blunders of my travels so far. As usual, we stayed up too late, and I bid Harue and Hideo goodnight and sent them off to their cabin.

The weather does not change drastically in the Indian Ocean. It was the middle of May, on a cool day, it was a pleasant coolness, and on a hot day, it was a bit hotter than midsummer in Japan. That evening the sky was blanketed by unusually dense clouds. The air was strangely oppressive and made you feel as though you were in a boiling kettle. I returned to my cabin, but thought a good night's sleep was impossible. I could have gone to the smoking room, but it was probably steaming in there, too. In the end, my curiosity took me up to the deck in the dead of night. A fresh breeze blew for a short time so I went out to the stern.

The hands of the clock had already turned to eleven o'clock. Not a soul other than the sailors on duty was on the expansive deck. The ship was advancing ten degrees north latitude cutting through the surging waves of the Indian Ocean. When we left the Port of Naples, the light of the *Crescent Moon* resembling a smile brightly lit the deck. But many days have passed, we had been gone for two weeks and the sky had been pitch black until recently. The faint line of a new moon could almost be discerned in the sky and had now fallen to the horizon. As far as I could see, the dark surface of the sea only reflected one or two points of starlight breaking through the dense clouds and unsteadily reflecting off the waves.

In this desolate scene, I was overcome by an indescribable sorrow. All people are sentient beings. When happy, they appear happy, and when sad, they feel sorrow. I was unexpectedly overcome by sadness about this melancholy scene. The many wild fantasies that lurked in my heart, and the ghost tales of the Devil's Hour and the Day of the Devil that persisted to this moment sprang to mind.

The dropping of the white masthead lights. The enraged face of the Captain. The binoculars on the mysterious ship. I vividly recalled the story about Naval Captain Sakuragi in the old newspaper, and the whereabouts of the sailing ship as if they were somehow connected to the night's grim scene.

"Stupid. How stupid!" I scolded myself. I forced those distractions out of my mind and purposely walked with arms swinging onto the deck. My ill feelings gradually diminished as I walked back and forth, four or five times between the foremast and the mizzen mast. I soon returned to my cabin to sleep, but as I was stepping down into the hatch, I heard peculiar echoes.

Distant echoes above the sea were barely audible, but were definitely reports of guns or explosive signal flares. I quickly turned my head to the port side, called out, and jumped back onto the deck. I noticed nothing earlier, but a glance revealed something rising above the sea about two or three nautical miles off the port quarter of the *Crescent Moon*. There was one faint report of gunfire, and burning of barrels of tar or oil formed raging flames on the sea. Simultaneously, two or three fiery shells shot into the air. Rockets resembling comets gradually streamed to the port and to the starboard sides. I was shocked. There shouldn't be any islands as far as you can see in the middle of the Indian Ocean. Rockets and explosive shells bursting for about one minute are the nighttime signals of a ship in distress to notify a life and death emergency.

"Oh! This is awful," I cried out as I looked to the port and the starboard of the ship.

Sailors were on duty to watch and constantly patrol in order to spot any of the multitude of incidents that occur at sea. At that moment, the sailors on watch on the starboard side moved toward the bow like wooden idols. They didn't appear to have heard the faint gunfire and were looking in the wrong direction. Without a doubt, the sailors on the port side saw the tragic distress signal of the rockets, but calmly stood by and only shielded their eyes.

Agitated, I cried out, "Men! Do something!"

I rushed to the Captain's quarters. Naturally, everyone knows the indisputable rules on a ship. The Law of the Sea states that it is absolutely inexcusable for a man who is not a sailor to infringe on the sailors' authority to inform the Captain of events, whether the skies are collapsing into thunderous skies or tens of thousands of evil spirits are simultaneously materializing above the sea. I was well aware of protocol, but this wasn't a simple emergency. In an instant, a ship in distress may be at the border between life and death. Also, the sailors on the starboard side of this ship seemed to be blinded and not know how to respond. I couldn't tell from their faces whether they had seen demons or serpents. I didn't have a moment to lose and ran at full speed to the Captain's quarters under the bridge and pounded on his door.

I screamed, "Captain! Captain! Wake up! There's an emergency! A ship's in distress!"

The Captain, who had been lying down on his sleeping berth, quickly got up, "What?! What?" he said and opened the door. I rushed into the cabin.

"Captain, I know this is not my place, but a ship may be in distress about three nautical miles off the port quarter."

"A ship in distress?! Oh, goodness."

The Captain laughed loudly. I thought he was surprised, but he immediately frowned in anger.

"A ship in distress? What is this? This ship always has a crew on duty scanning the seas. There is no reason for you to concern yourself."

"Of course, but the watch sailors on this ship don't have eyes nor feelings. One is dumb struck. Another acts like he doesn't know what to do. Captain, the fate of a ship in distress is a fight against time."

"Stop!" The Captain laughed coldly.

"Do you not understand the Law of the Sea? Here's an example. If an incident occurs, no one other that a sailor has the right to intervene. Moreover, I am under no obligation to accept a report from the likes of you."

He was wagging his right hand at me as he picked up a cigar on his desk.

Impatient, I said, "Be reasonable. Exceeding my authority is my burden. Don't you believe me? Right now, a ship is in distress and seeking aid."

"I don't believe you. I can't believe you."

The Captain angrily slapped the cigar back down on the desk.

"I believe nothing as long as a sailor on watch has not made a report. Furthermore, nothing should be in distress on this calm sea."

"Dammit," I seethed. My chronic quick temper briefly exploded.

"What do you mean 'nothing.' I came here as a witness."

"Ha ha ha... What did you witness? Ha ha ha."

He feigned ignorance and roared with laughter. My fury reignited. As I've said, when I first boarded this ship, one look at the Captain told me that he was not a principled man. Now, he intended to spare himself the trouble of being a witness to the peril of the other ship. I was incensed.

"I saw nothing. Well, isn't the first rocket shot in explosive shells striking the sea off the port quarter of this ship a signal of a ship in distress?"

"There is no need to inform me about that kind of event," the Captain snorted in laughter.

"Perhaps, your eyes were playing tricks on you. How about that?"

"My eyes tricked me? That is an insult. I have perfect vision."

"Eyes are mysterious and are often dazzled by the sea. You undoubtedly saw a meteor in flight," he said as he jutted out his barrel-shaped chest.

He nonchalantly added, "No, what if these were truly distress signals? A ship wrecked on this placid sea is not in the experience of my sailors. They saw nothing that troubled their eyes and are not obligated to attempt a rescue."

Soon I understood the futility of going back and forth with questions and answers and yanked the Captain out of his cabin.

"Can't you see that? Doesn't that look like the light of a distress signal?" I pointed to a distant point above the sea in the port quarter direction, but only exclaimed, "Ah!"

Something was wrong.

The fiery light of the scintillating distress signals flying in the air from two or three minutes earlier had vanished. I only saw a white bulb shining about several dozen feet above the ocean surface at that spot, and the lights from green and red lamps at positions apparently on the starboard and port sides of a ship. Needless to say, the white lamp was at the foremast, the green light on the port side, and the red light on the starboard side, the signal for safe navigation.

"Aah, of course, a first rocket shot in explosive shells and the signal of a ship in distress seeking help are clearly visible. Your eyes are quite good."

The ill-tempered Captain glared at my face. I said nothing. But wasn't this strange? The signals of a tragic ship in distress had been visible in the region of the sea where safe navigation lights were now shining. My eyes were probably at fault as the Captain had said.

No. No. As I thought about it, I concluded that my eyes were not so bad that I could mistake the light from the white, green, and red lamps for explosive shells and rockets. Without question, that earlier distress signal was changed at some time to safe navigation. I was unable to explain this and at a loss for the moment.

The Captain glared at me with venom for a time and

laughed scornfully, but became somewhat solemn as he looked at the lights.

"However, this is strange. According to this month's nautical chart, around this time, there shouldn't be any ships following my ship in this sea lane."

He cocked his head and chuckled. He muttered to himself, "Oh! Now, I understand. Dammit. Things are not going well. The marine spirit of the Turk that sank in this area mimicked a ship in distress that is unable to float in order to draw this ship into a reef. Wait a minute! None of your tricks!"

He addressed me, "But earlier you could see the distress signals of a ship actually seeking help?"

He wasn't sincere. Strangely, many ship passengers do embrace superstition. I did not take notice and simply answered, "Yes, it was undoubtedly the distress signal of a ship seeking help!"

He only said, "Well, I'm certain it was simply a marine spirit."

He dismissed everything I had said.

When I scanned the ocean, the three lamp lights I saw were not lights cast off by some unworldly entity, like a vengeful ghost or a sea phantom, as the half-witted Captain had said. Both the green and red lights were definitely the sidelights of a ship. The white light high above the sea was the masthead light more than twenty feet above the deck, as stipulated by the Law of the Sea. That ship was pursuing the *Crescent Moon*.

7

PIRATES OF THE INDIAN OCEAN

As **I stared intently**, the ship with a green light on the starboard side, a red light on the port side, and a scintillating white light on the foremast twenty feet above the deck gradually inched closer in the darkness of the Indian Ocean. The *Crescent Moon* was advancing at a speed of twelve or thirteen knots, so a ship rapidly closing in from behind must have been moving at an astonishing speed. In today's world, a ship having such remarkable speed could only be a destroyer or a cruiser armed with torpedoes. The formation of those lights probably indicated a type of warship. If it was a warship, I wasn't concerned yet about what type, maybe it was a...but an unexpected memory made me shudder.

Although I still hadn't identified the ship, my concern may have been ridiculous, but that ship's strange behavior earlier was disconcerting. First, mimicking a ship in distress by exploding shells and launching rockets above the black sea in the distance was simply dismissed by the insipid words of the Captain as the work of a marine spirit. The signal from this mystery ship was the deed of some entity perhaps one hundred or one thousand times more fearsome than a sea phantom, or a marine spirit not of this world. What could their intentions be?

Was it to lure the *Crescent Moon* to that part of the ocean? In fact, no voyage is as terrifying as a voyage on the Indian Ocean. Typhoons, gale-force winds, impenetrable sea fog, as well as the horrors of surges and reverse tidal waves, and freakish nimbus and cumulus clouds are hard to avoid on any voyage and are hardships on the sailors. Aside from these hardships, the most terrifying calamity on the Indian Ocean is a raid by a pirate ship.

On this ocean long ago, hundreds, maybe thousands, of ships were attacked by pirate ships and met a tragic end. The oceans are not as infested today with pirate ships as recounted in the old tales, but the pirate ships of old did not attack and sink the targeted cargo ship in a single blow, they always boarded the other ship. Many armed pirates brandishing swords leaped onto the deck of the other ship. Both sides fought to win as they spilled each other's blood. If the pirate's won, needless to say, I cannot speak of the devastating scene. However, if their opponent triumphed, the pirates would face execution.

Today, however, this step is rarely taken. Pirates are cunning. Since the invention of deep-sea diving equipment, many pirate ships have made use of these devices. If a ship loaded with riches of gold and silver was identified on the vast sea, that ship would be sent to the ocean floor in a single blow by a gun or a ram. Later, the pirates would submerge diving equipment to retrieve the riches.

Of course, even today, the invention of diving equipment has not yet been perfected, so obviously this tactic cannot always be used. Even with today's best diving equipment, the water pressure at depths above fifty meters causes the air pumps to malfunction and makes using the equipment impossible. Thus, a pirate ship using diving equipment must always be alert. On an ocean with raging swells, the targeted cargo ship should not be sunk at places deeper than fifty meters, but near an island or crossing over an open-sea reef. Surrounded by the black Indian Ocean, this thought suddenly came to mind when I observed that mysterious ship trailing the *Crescent Moon*.

You may laugh, dear reader, and believe that my concerns are just nerves. However, if you consider both this story and the distress signal mysteriously raised a few minutes ago by that ship trailing on the starboard side of our ship, some concern is not unreasonable. I am not well versed in the conditions on the floor of the Indian Ocean, but in an area of 2.5 million square miles, there are unfathomable depths, as well as, places crossing over submerged rocks or reefs no deeper than fifty meters. Considering this, I may not be wrong, this vision may come to pass. This mysterious ship trailing our ship was a great demon of the Indian Ocean and a notorious pirate ship. For some reason, the sea floor in that area may not have been deep enough for diving. By setting off explosive shells and rockets to mimic distress and seek help in a more suitable place on this immense ocean, the ship could submerge and use the diving equipment after sinking the *Crescent Moon*.

The ignorant captain of this ship foolishly said, "The marine spirit mimicked a ship in distress...in order to draw this ship into a reef."

However, an actual pirate ship and not a marine spirit may have designs to lure this ship into an area with a reef. The *Crescent Moon* happened to ignore the signal and continued its rapid advance. Therefore, the pirate ship's plan had been foiled, and it had to prepare another plan and fervently pursue us. Unfortunately, if I am correct, a horrible event will ensue.

We were still separated from the mysterious ship by over one nautical mile. I deduced the tremendous speed of that ship from the gradually brightening of its white light. Before long, maybe ten, maybe fifteen minutes from now, the ship would be upon us.

Oh, is it a pirate ship? A pirate ship? If that ship were a notorious pirate ship of the Indian Ocean, the fate of the *Crescent Moon* being watched by that ship would soon unfold. If our ship tried to flee under full sail with fires blazing until the steam engine broke down, we may be able to escape.

Naturally, if that ship were a pirate ship, as I imagined, it may recklessly attack and sink us. The average depth of the Indian Ocean is 1,830 fathoms. If we are attacked and sunk to such a depth, that ship could not possibly achieve its objective. However, if that pirate ship deceives fearsome evil spirits, how could they overlook a ship once spied?

Mulling over our dilemma, one weapon of a pirate ship as told in the old tales was to charge their sharp bow straight at us. The monstrous pirates brandishing weapons would jump onto our deck like an ominous rain cloud. Perhaps that ship would slip in and out of view as it leisurely trailed our ship. At the moment our ship passed in the shallow waters near an island or passed over waves crossing an open-sea reef on the bottom, it would come like the wind and emerge like a cloud, resolved to attack and sink our ship right there in a single blow. Thinking about this worsened my mood. I felt a chill from the depths of my soul.

Nevertheless, the mysterious ship slowly approached. About four or five hundred meters from the port quarter of our ship, the white, red, and green lights glinted in the dark night, like the huge eyes of a demon.

My heart pounded as I surveyed the entire deck. At

that time, the barrel-chested Captain was standing on the ship's bridge above me, as is his custom, and often stared in the direction of the mystery ship. Although he vaguely recognized the three lights on the vast ocean earlier and said nothing was there, as things now stood, he was no longer uttering such inane statements.

"Well now, that's odd. Isn't that a steamship? Maybe it was mistakenly left off this month's nautical chart," he said as he gazed up at the starlit sky.

"No. No. There is no way that that ship should be following us in this sea lane at this time." He looked to be on edge.

Many sailors from throughout the ship had already gathered near the bridge. All looked with amazement and suspicion at the lights of the unknown ship creeping toward us.

The first mate peered out and glanced at the chronometer in his right hand lit by the ship's lights.

"That's strange...that ship's making headway fast."

"I wonder what company made that steamship."

"Is it a merchant ship? A mail boat?"

"Nope, it's definitely a warship."

"Even if it is a warship, a ship that fast could only be a new cruiser or a destroyer armed with torpedoes," said the second mate.

Even the off-duty steersmen, fire stokers, and cabin boys were skittish, looking at each other and cursing. Some of them had seen the earlier mysterious signals, some had not. The mystery ship was abreast with the *Crescent Moon*.

The Captain on the bridge looked around and often seemed anxious. The first mate quickly ran to the stern and immediately shouted a command. A signalman raised a white light high on the starboard side and stood on the deck on the port quarter. By the Law of the Sea, this was the nighttime signal displayed when a ship is on the verge of being overtaken by another ship. However, that mysterious ship did not answer this signal, but instantly lit up the sky with a lone dazzling searchlight. A blinding light was thrown onto our deck. They sounded one or two blasts of an air whistle, and kicked up the waves as they sped ahead. As I watched, the white masthead light of the mystery ship line up with the masthead light of the *Crescent Moon*. Soon, their starboard-side green light was ahead of our port-side red light. One meter...two meters...three meters, if we had been a boat, they would have already passed us by more than a half length.

The time had come!

I could not make out the profile of the mystery ship. I turned and ran to the port bow to get a better look. With no moon and few stars, the surface of the ocean was pitch black for one to two hundred meters. I could see one point of light at the head of the foremast and the red light on the port side. The green light on the starboard side of the ship resembled a giant eye of a venomous snake. The ship having no flickering lights visible from the bridge, the deck, nor the porthole was shrouded in darkness. Perhaps it was my nerves being piqued somewhat in my zeal or my pupils adjusting to the darkness, but just as I was able to make out the form of that light, that area was again illuminated by the searchlight. In the sudden brightness, I yelled out at a sight so shocking I almost fainted.

"*Sea Snake*! The *Sea Snake*!"

Do you recall that name? When the *Crescent Moon* was leaving the Port of Naples, I spotted that mysterious ship. A 1,000-ton class ship with two masts and two funnels, and a lower deck filled with cannons and rifles. I barely recognized that ship that seemed suspiciously fast and deeply sunk into the black waves.

"Without a doubt, that's the *Sea Snake*," I cried out again. The *Sea Snake* had behaved queerly when it left the Port of Naples. Despite exiting several minutes before the *Crescent Moon* and being a swift vessel, it had been following us. Was this simply a coincidence?

Until now, however, the *Sea Snake* never exhibited any malice. She had always sent out a searchlight from its deck to illuminate the sky, shined the light toward us, searched the geographical features on the sea, and lit the waves of the sea line traveled by the *Crescent Moon*. She rapidly left us behind, and now our ship was trailing her.

About ten minutes later, the two ships were far apart. I absentmindedly rubbed by chest and wondered, "Was my worrying unfounded?" I suddenly realized that the *Crescent Moon* earlier enveloped in an extreme tranquility had over time become so agitated that the deck was almost tipping. As I stared out, the waves kicking up from the unusually rough black sea resembled white horses. The Indian Ocean doesn't only have great depth, it has places like this with turbulent standing waves that may be crossing a giant reef, and places where the bottom of the sea route followed by the *Crescent Moon* may be covered by an open-sea reef.

A giant reef! An open-sea reef! The sea is known to be shallow in areas like these, though not enough to strand a ship. At that moment, I heard alarmed shouts coming from the forecastle deck of the *Crescent Moon*. I leaped up to look. Already at least one nautical mile away, the *Sea Snake* had been shining a bright light in all directions on the sea and was now shining it on the sea in front of our bow. The light abruptly went out. As I watched, the ship rapidly turned and charged toward us.

"Hey! What's going on!" My heart pounded.

I wasn't the only one who was alarmed. The Captain on the bridge, the first mate on the quarterdeck, the second mate, the third mate, the sailors, the fire stokers, and the lookouts all paled and came running to the forecastle deck. The distance between the *Sea Snake* rushing directly toward us and the *Crescent Moon* rapidly shrunk to less than one thousand meters. While still a good distance away, the sea route of the steamship was narrow. This wasn't like the Ravenna incident at the Kurile Islands where even the slightest steering error would result in a horrible crash. We had a bigger problem. For some reason, the mysterious *Sea Snake* was pointed at the *Crescent Moon* and charging toward us on the same route. Our destiny was a horrific collision, one minute, two minutes, or maybe three minutes from now.

The Captain and the first mate dashed up and down the bridge in a panic, ran to the quarterdeck, and leaped onto the forecastle deck, all while yelling at the top of their lungs.

The sailors, fire stokers, and cabin boys had not yet sunk into confusion. The passengers, more awake than asleep, were running out onto the deck wondering what was going on. "Get out of the way!" The passengers were jostled by two or three sailors as they turned out of the hatchway. Our ship was launching exploding signals one after another, and was about to sound the emergency alarm and to ring the signal bell to warn of danger. However, the *Sea Snake* only hurled toward us in silence.

The helmsman of our ship frantically steered left and right, but to no avail. If we gave one short blast of air for starboard, the *Sea Snake* concealed the red port light as she took the starboard route. If we gave two short blasts for port, she revealed her red port light as she took the port route. Nothing could be more suspicious. The *Sea Snake* kicked up turbulent waves in the shallow waters. They planned to sink the *Crescent Moon* with a single blow.

"We're gonna collide! She's gonna hit us!" cries were heard from the one hundred or so mesmerized sailors on deck. The *Sea Snake* was less than two hundred and twenty or thirty meters from us. In desperation, the first mate and the Captain screamed, "Full power reverse! Reverse! Reverse!"

Simultaneously, our ship spat out three short blasts of air, the steam engined turned over, and foamy bubbles formed near the propeller as it reversed rotation. I think the ship was able to pull back twenty or thirty meters, but it was too late. The *Sea Snake* was less than one hundred meters from the lateral front of the *Crescent Moon*. Unexpectedly, their bow appeared to be turning to the port side, the sharp ram aimed for the middle of our ship and in an instant hit us. The *Crescent Moon* crumbled and listed to the port side. Loud screams erupted. Two hundred distraught sailors frantically ran around the deck. Several hundred passengers materialized like a black cloud.

Like the wind and like a flash of lightning, the *Sea Snake* came. And like the wind and like a flash of lightning, the *Sea Snake* disappeared between the waves of the black sea.

The sky revealed one, two, perhaps three specks of light. The winds died down. The waves blackened. In seconds, pandemonium engulfed the ship. The *Crescent Moon* was sinking to the bottom of the Indian Ocean.

8

———

THE FATE OF HUMANITY

N**othing is more mysterious** than the fate of humanity. The day after this singular event, the lives of Hideo and me were entrusted to a small lifeboat not even thirty feet long drifting on the waves of this vast expanse of sea of water and air. Of course, the *Crescent Moon* filled with unrestrained anger had sunk to the bottom of the Indian Ocean.

If people on a grassy green shore in a soft breeze heard about a ship sinking, they would think of it as a curious event or draw in their hearts a tragic scene of assorted incidents in some drama or oil painting. As I pondered this misfortune, my hairs stood on end thinking about those poor souls who remained on deck until the miserable end of the *Crescent Moon* and were now gone forever. I can't bear to tell the story in detail, but here I will sketch out only what must be told.

After the *Sea Snake* crashed into the starboard side of the *Crescent Moon* and faded into the darkness like the wind, the tumult onboard the ship resembled a kettle boiling over. Shrieks, cries, voices pleading for help melded into a horrid, heartbreaking sound, a scene from Hell.

Although every possible attempt was made to hold the water back, the water spray cascaded in from below the draft like a waterfall of seawater. The area couldn't be reached. The ten-year-old pumps disgorged water at full power, but to no effect. The huge 6,400-ton ship was already listing forty-five degrees. The thick black smoke belching from the two funnels seemed like complaints against the agonies at the threshold of death.

"It's no use! She's going to sink!"

The sailors had already abandoned the ship to its fate. Up to that moment, I was stunned by the tragic situation. My eyes absorbed the dreadful scene as I rose up at one end of the deck, but I soon snapped out of this trance.

"What's happened to Harue and Hideo?"

I flew toward their cabin. I chanced upon them near the hatch where they had just come up. Harue had been awakened by the sudden commotion. Despite the urgency, she never forgot her modesty. Only after she changed from her night clothes into her dress clothes did she make her way to this spot.

"Harue, something has happened."

"What? A sunken reef?" she asked sorrowfully.

"A sunken reef? What? Hurry!" I urged her to come quickly and grabbed the surprised Hideo, who only stared, and led them to the deck. A place crowded with people in turmoil was dangerous. The three of us left them and went to the side of the chart house at the bow.

I was first struck by my firm promise to Hamajima when we left the Port of Naples for the open sea. I promised to keep his wife and beloved child safe even if the cost was my life. We now faced an emergency, and my life must be dedicated to saving them. The ship was sinking with each passing second, and the screams and shouts from the deck had become frenzied. The order came, "Lower the lifeboats!" The first lifeboat was lowered onto the waves. I looked back at Harue.

"Harue, we should prepare to evacuate."

From all Laws of the Sea, the first lifeboats lowered are for first-class passengers, followed by second-class passengers, and third-class passengers. Any boats remaining after all of the passengers have escaped are provided to the sailors for their escape.

Having rights as first-class passengers, I went down to the first lifeboat and summoned Harue and Hideo. Naturally, if I had been ill-bred, I would never have been able to flee first as the only Japanese man. However, I had sworn to my friend to keep Harue and Hideo safe. I was quite anxious, worried that the delicate Harue and the innocent Hideo would be unable to flee. But my efforts were in vain. Whether the first lifeboat would float on these waves was in question. And instantly several hundred souls rushed in like an avalanche. When they boarded the lifeboat before us, we were driven back by the surging crowd as if swept back by the winds of a black cloud. I took a few steps forward and turned, "Harue, this is no good." How could Harue and Hideo safely board that lifeboat in this insane, unruly throng?

In moments of peril, people have neither shame nor honor. I sighed and stared at these people whose lives were so precious. Strangely, the group who launched themselves into the lifeboat were not the first-class passengers nor the second-class passengers. They were those who should have stood their ground, the sailors, the firemen, the helmsmen, the engineers, and a band of scummy low-class passengers. Through brute strength, they swept aside and kicked others to board the lifeboat before us.

"What disgraceful behavior!"

I was disheartened. Behind me, Harue simply hugged her dear child in silence. She was truly the wife of the formidable Hamajima Takebumi and the younger sister of Captain Matsushima of the Imperial Navy. She wasn't the least bit distraught and seemed to have already surrendered her fate to heaven. Witnessing such commendable behavior, I could not remain silent.

"Hey, you! Sailors! You fools! Cowardly foreigners! Remember the Law of the Sea!"

When I grabbed someone's despicable arm, Harue's sorrowful face turned to me and in a voice filled with despair said, "Stop. Everyone wants to save his own life." She averted her eyes and added, "And a boat so full will sink."

She had forgotten about the danger to herself, instead she was concerned about others. Trying to sound encouraging, I turned and yelled, "Harue, that's not so. I must save you and the boy. I'm not done."

When I turned around, the second lifeboat had been lowered as well as the third. However, the crowd had swelled. I could only stamp my foot in frustration.

Soon the Captain who bore responsibility for this ship caught my eye. He was still a coward. He boarded the third lifeboat and abandoned several hundred passengers near the sidelights as they cried to heaven while their tears fell to the ground.

"You...you damn coward!"

I was frantic. How could the captain behave so deplorably in the presence of praiseworthy women like Harue? I could no longer remain silent. My next action would be more pointless than my earlier ones. Although filled with rage, I was unable to introduce my clenched fist to his head. Harue had quietly clutched my sleeve.

"There is nothing left to do. Even if Hideo and I disappear into watery graves in this sea, I don't believe a rescue should be carried out unwillingly?" It would be like a fern complaining to the rain. She fondly gazed at the face of her dear son.

"But if there is a gift from God, we may sink beneath the waves, or we may be saved," she looked up to the sky, her eyes brimming with tears.

Screams abruptly rose from the dark sea. They seemed to be coming from the many people who had escaped from the ship on one or two of the lifeboats.

"Oh, how cruel," said Harue, and covered her face with a handkerchief.

"Serves them right." I said under my breath, unable to suppress a sneer.

The fate of the *Crescent Moon* was one or two minutes away. Not one lifeboat remained on deck. Now, escape was unthinkable. Our only hope was a praiseworthy demise.

"Harue," I quietly called. "Everything is destiny. However, even as we face this unexpected disaster, I am satisfied if, in the very least, we do not damage the honor of our Japan," I said.

Harue nodded slightly, overwhelmed, she kissed the rosy cheeks of her son and said, "Hideo, even if we meet disaster soon, you won't forget the words of Papa when we left Naples."

The look on Hideo's face was inspiring.

"I remember. Papa patted my head and said, 'Never forget you are a Japanese child.'"

Tears flowed unchecked from Harue's eyes.

My final words were, "You and your mother may leave this place forever. If by some fortune, your life is saved, when you make your mark in this world, never forget these words and live as an honorable man."

Soon, raging waves shot up from the stern. The end was near. My eyes darted around in desperation and locked onto a couple of buoys in a heap on the port side. In their mad rush to the lifeboats, everyone had overlooked them. I snatched them up and quickly passed one to Harue and another to Hideo.

Just as the ship sounded like Heaven and Earth ripping apart and began to sink to the ocean floor, I could only say, "Hideo," and grabbed the nape of his neck with my left hand.

For a moment, the 6,400-ton *Crescent Moon* floated again on the black sea, but was soon engulfed by foaming waves, a swirling vortex, and a bottomless fury, then she was gone. I was surrounded only by voices pleading for help. I had lost my buoy, but luckily I was still holding onto Hideo's right hand. I had also lost sight of Harue.

"Harue! Harue!" I shouted with all my might, but no answer came.

Once, I thought I heard a faint reply from some far off waves. Was it the sounds of the waves or a trick of my mind? I couldn't see anything resembling Harue's figure. I never feared drowning because I could swim quite a distance since childhood. I held Hideo close, and we were only dunked once thanks to the strength of that lone buoy. We were some distance from where the *Crescent Moon* sank and could no longer hear voices crying for help. Suddenly Hideo yelled, "Over there. There's a black thing over there."

I raised my head and was shocked by the sight of a lifeboat floating about fourteen or fifteen yards in front of us. However, that boat was probably overloaded with people and about to capsize. As we neared, it became clear that not a single soul was on the boat, which was half filled with seawater. At that instant, I asked heaven for any help.

I swam to the side of the boat and furiously bailed out the seawater, as Hideo held onto the buoy. Around daybreak the water was emptied out. We got into the boat, and with no destination we drifted on the waves of the Indian Ocean.

9

———

A SMALL LIFEBOAT ON A VAST SEA

At last, the terrifying night ended. A faint glow radiated from the eastern sky. The soft morning light shining above us from the horizon was no different than yesterday's. However, our lot had transformed completely. Until yesterday, we lived in the luxurious cabins of the *Crescent Moon*, awoke each morning and ran out to the deck, as a cool dawn breeze blew. Now we only saw the frightful surface of the sea we had previously gazed at with pleasure. Engulfed by the boundless sea spray of the Indian Ocean as far as we could see and with neither sails nor oars, we could only drift on the waves in this small lifeboat entrusted with our lives. As I pondered the events of last evening, it all seemed like a dream.

"Why did we meet such misfortune?"

Last night, I was dumped into the sea and am now completely drenched and shivering in a cold wind.

Hideo was hugging his knees. I touched my hand to my heart as I stared at the surface of waves that looked forlorn as the sun briefly hid behind the drifting clouds. The god of misfortune seemed to have haunted us from the start of this voyage. Incidents like the crashing of the white mast-head light when we left port, and the drowning of a passenger in the Strait of Messina seemed like heaven's will and may have presaged our peril. No. It is not something so stupid. But Annie's tears at the wharf in Naples somehow hit the mark. Naturally, I did not believe there was any link to Devil's Hour on the Day of the Devil, but the old woman's final words, "And all that gold and pearls gathered on the *Crescent Moon*, which I heard about from a friendly sailor, on the rough waves of the sea is a terrifying curse." Her prediction had come to pass. For these treasures, we suffered an attack last night by the fearsome pirates and the devils of the Indian Ocean. Our ship was sunk. Harue was lost. And with no hope of rescue, our fates had become the pitiful ephemeral fate of foam tossed on the waves. As I thought about it, I became more dispirited and had no will to live. Meanwhile, brilliant sunlight radiated through breaks in the clouds.

The innocent Hideo was trapped in this situation. Unable to bear the exhaustion of last night, he was leaning against my knees peacefully asleep. Suddenly, these sleep-talking words slipped from his cherubic lips.

"Oh, Mama you left me. Where are you? Aaah, a beautiful bridge between Naples and Mount Fuji. Oh, Papa is calling my name."

In his dreams, he is with his beloved father and mother. He was in some way connected by the dream to his adored father Hamajima Takebumi in far off Naples. Harue, the mother he longed for in his dreams, had fallen into the sea last night and was lost. If heaven possesses extraordinary wisdom, she may have been rescued unharmed. But if she was swallowed by the sea and her soul returned to heaven, our fortune may improve, and we will be rescued. Perhaps, Hideo can only see the face of his dear mother in a dream.

As I had these thoughts, I felt unbearable sorrow, and my tears fell onto Hideo's cheek and woke him. He saw my tear-stained face and asked, "Oh, Uncle what's the matter?"

I quickly regained my composure and laughed loudly.

"What? No, nothing Hideo. You were asleep and I was little lonely. I was simply yawning."

The boy rubbed his eyes and looked around the boat, as sad as anyone could be. After an extraordinary change, you drift off into your dreams for a short time, and when you reawaken, the loneliness is gone. This eight-year-old boy had been thrust into this predicament. When he remembered the figure of his kind mother and his father in distant Naples, he was surely in deep despair. He looked around the pitiful lifeboat that had neither a crumb of bread nor a scrap of meat. I couldn't describe how pitiful he looked gazing at my face.

My pocket watch had been soaked in seawater and was now useless. I guessed the time to be between ten and eleven in the morning. I suddenly realized that this boat I thought was merely drifting on the waves was being accelerated like an arrow by some unknown force and gliding from the northeast to the southwest.

I didn't have a compass, but I could determine our heading from the position of the sun. I was surprised for a moment, but after thinking about it, there was no mystery at all. I hadn't noticed until now because there was nothing to look at. This is often the case on the surface of the vast sea with no frame of reference, like an island or a ship. At some point, our boat would be pulled into the well-known spring tidal currents.

At last, I felt some hope. These currents flow without fail from the direction of the Laccadive islands, past the west coast of the Indian continent, approach close to the island of Madagascar, and toward the southern coast of Africa. In this case, I thought we may be spotted and rescued by a steamship or drift into a trading port of some country. However, how often do things go as you think they should in this world? These tidal currents could go directly to the coast of Africa and the South Pacific where there are many dangerous places. The currents could take us to the land of cannibals or to a pirate island. That would be horrible! I couldn't stop wondering what would happen. Our fate was in God's hands!

The skies had been clear until now, but as I looked, clouds were drawing near from the west. We were caught in one of those famous torrential rainfalls of the tropics. The ocean surface looked like the basin of a waterfall. The downpour was severe at times and soaked us. We buried our heads in the bottom of the boat. Our seawater-logged clothes from last night that had just dried were drenched again.

Heaven had been merciless. I glared at the black clouds for a moment, intent on cursing heaven. But after a little thought, everything in this world has moments of disaster and of bliss. Only at that time, I didn't realize that.

Soon after the torrential downpour came a time to be grateful for the favor of heaven. The rain soon stopped, and we were bathed in radiant sunlight. The rays of sun after rain in the Indian Ocean were spectacular, but I thought about dying of thirst. That was the first time I felt the unbearable pangs of thirst. Usually, this is the time to talk about turning misfortune into fortune. The first challenge of a castaway is to find fresh water. However, eight or nine out of ten times, they will fail and die. Fortunately, we avoided this hardship. The rainwater that poured down earlier like a waterfall had accumulated in the bottom of the boat. Needless to say, it was tepid and rancid.

I scooped up some water with both hands and drank like a cow. My thirst was quenched, but the hunger pangs came. If I had known about this when we leaped into the sea last night, I would have shoved a tin of biscuits in my clothes. There's no room for regret now. Last night's warm soup, light brown fries, and warm roasted chicken were making their way to my esophagus. Not only that, I was mortified when I recalled long ago screaming in anger because the grilled meat was a little burnt and fed it to a dog, and saying that a sandwich was a luxury in a work-man's lunch and tossed it out the window of a steam engine.

That day I was famished. That night I dreamt only of food. The next day, the hunger intensified. Both the boy and I were ashen and simply looked at each other. Even the foolish thought of pulverizing and eating the wood on the sides of the boat crossed my mind. Night fell. The bottom of the boat was my pillow, but my empty stomach kept me awake all night.

The agonizing night ended, and the sun rose again. I promptly got up, but didn't have the courage to welcome the light of the morning sun. Hideo was already sitting up, surveying the sea. Suddenly, he screamed, "A fish! A giant fish!"

10

A SHARK'S BURIAL AT SEA

S**tartled by the boy**, I looked out at the sea and shouted, "We're in the Sea of Sharks!"

The Sea of Sharks is a peculiar, but famous name. It is said to be located several thousand miles south of the Maldives archipelago in the Indian Ocean. I was now looking out at a place I had once read about in a geography book. The small sharks were about four or five feet long, and the large ones twenty to thirty feet long. They had formed a school and rushed to the vicinity of our boat.

Sharks are savage fish. No doubt, they approached to see whether we were a favorite meal. Seeing the school immediately gave me purpose. Stabbed by hunger pangs, I wondered what could I use to snag one of them. Unfortunately, I had nothing, no net, no fishing gear, just a goal. Without warning, a small fish leaped up between the waves and hurled itself into our boat. Hideo pounced on it like a kitten.

"It got away," I said in frustration. But when he turned over, I was delighted. The fish, a horse mackerel, was about a foot long. It was being chased by the school of fish and fortuitously jumped into our boat. I quickly snatched up this gift from heaven. In fact, for both the boy and me, a mere mouthful would satisfy our unbearable hunger. Wait! What would happen if we devoured this small fish right now in a frenzy? Even when hungry, a peasant plans for the year by planting rather than eating a cup of barley. I also had a plan to multiply this small fish one hundred, no two hundred times. I thought about capturing that large shark with this small mackerel. I explained my plan to Hideo, and he fully agreed.

Of course, I didn't have any fishing gear. Fortunately, the strong iron chain used to lash this lifeboat to the ship and the attached hook remained. I removed the hook, impaled the mackerel on it, and I slowly stood up. I wasn't worried about whether I'd catch a fish because the fish in this vast, distant sea never encounter fishermen. But I feared that a huge fish would capsize the boat. At that instant, a shark, three or four feet long, swam near the starboard side. "That's the one," I said. Would he go down into the waves for the bait?

"Aw! Dammit!" I shouted.

Survival of the fittest is inescapable even for fish in the sea. An astonishingly enormous fish was at the bottom of the wave where a small shark was swimming. In a flash, the larger one propelled its body upward and swallowed my hook.

The currents frothed instantly, and the waves spiraled in reverse, like a tsunami was looming. I clung with all my strength to the iron chain, but my slim chances troubled me. Of course, even if this giant fish didn't struggle, pulling him in would be no easy task. Any mistake would pull us down with the boat to the bottom of the sea. But at that moment, the chain loosened somehow. Had the shark won? Had I lost? Catching or not catching this fish would be the decisive moment between life and death. Hideo's eyes were wide open in amazement as he took in this hair-raising sight. His small figure had wrapped his arms around me from behind.

"You're in danger!! I'll help!" he yelled.

"What!? No! I'm okay! I'm okay!"

I flushed red as I towered over him like a guardian god. Meanwhile, the shark raged in all directions. With his repulsive head pointed south, he took off like an arrow, dragging the boat along. This was do or die.

"You're not getting away that easily!"

I forgot about everything, my empty stomach and the danger to my life. In any case, that crazed shark dragged us around for nearly three hours. I didn't notice we had escaped the tidal currents until we were about fourteen or fifteen nautical miles away from the Sea of Sharks. The savage fish was exhausted. Its white belly floated on the surface of the sea. I sighed with relief and hauled it into the boat. This fish was bigger than I thought and filled up almost half the boat.

"Wow, what an ugly fish," said Hideo looking anxious as he punched the shark's hard head.

"Ha ha ha. That was tough, but now we don't have to worry about starving to death," I said to Hideo and immediately pulled out my knife. A shark isn't a tasty fish, but in this case, no matter how much we ate, it wasn't enough.

A little concerned, I warned, "Hideo, if you eat too much, you'll damage your stomach."

Nevertheless, we crammed the fishy-smelling flesh into our mouths. This huge catch erased any concern about starving to death, at least for a while. To be honest, I slept peacefully that night and woke up the following day feeling unusually relaxed. That day was the first time since we were cast adrift I could relax. We drank ordinary rainwater and ate the shark meat with relish.

We were always watchful for the silhouette of an island or the smoke from a steamship, but nothing interrupted our view. On that day, we only gazed on the surface of the vast blue expanse. At least, the shark had dragged our boat out of the tidal currents. Instead, we were now in a reverse current. This time we were moving east from the southwest and being carried south of the Maldives archipelago. Just as I realized we were being sucked into a swifter, stronger tidal current, I unintentionally cried out, surprised by the sight some distance away of a huge pod of whales, like I had once read about in a book. But other than that, nothing changed. Of course, our present circumstance had its problems, but our bellies had ample strength and we were invigorated.

Under the sun's brilliant warm light, Hideo stared at my face, "Hey Uncle, I just realized you're black."

You can't see your own face. Yesterday's handsome young man was now sunburned as well as windburned by the salty breeze. Hideo pointed and laughed at my cluelessness of looking like the eldest son of a charcoal brick maker. Trying times do have humorous moments.

The sun set and returned the next day. We did not see the dot of an island's silhouette nor smoke from a steamship on the surface of the ocean where the water turns into the sky. However, a major event did occur. That shark meat, our lifeline, had begun to slowly rot. I was a little worried about this from the start, but neglected to do anything to prevent the unusually large fish from rapidly spoiling. And on the morning of the fifth day, I was rudely reminded. I said nothing this time and bravely ate, but it was unbearable after having been constantly baked by the scorching heat of the Indian Ocean. At lunchtime, the innocent boy took one bite and promptly spit the meat into the sea.

"Yuck, this is awful. The fish tastes bad," he cried out.

This situation was disheartening. When evening came, although I eventually found courage, I didn't have the heart to eat. Yet, I couldn't bear to merely toss that important lifeline into the sea. I pushed it away to the furthest corner of the boat. Our miserable state of four or five days ago had returned. When another night passed and the next morning came, the stench was unbearable. As the air and the spirit grew faint, it was difficult to live with the decayed fish one more second and drink in its eternal grudge. Together, the boy and I buried the corpse of the shark in the depths of the sea.

We had no food again. The day ended idly and night fell. I wondered what would happen next. In despair and filled with anxiety, I was unable to sleep the entire night. Morning came. A gentle dawn breeze blew, and the eastern sky faintly glowed. I lacked the courage to rise and unintentionally yelled, "It's no use. Our food is gone. I can't see any steamships. And there are no islands."

When I realized Hideo was sleeping peacefully beside me and glanced at him, I saw that I had startled him out of his slumber and he got up grumpy. He leaned half his body out of the boat and in a surprisingly cheerful voice said, "An island! An island! Uncle, I can see an island!"

"An island?"

When I leaped up as if playing a game of *kemari* to take a look, the sky was clear and just three nautical miles south of our boat through the clear morning mist on the surface of the sea, a single island spread out before us with luxuriant coconut palm fronds and olive leaves. The waves hitting its beach broke into jewels.

11

ECHOES ON A DESERT ISLAND

From a distance, the island resembled a calf in repose and seemed quite large. Nearly a dozen days had passed since the *Crescent Moon* sank, we had been looking at nothing but blue sky and blue waves. We were elated by the discovery of this island and would have flown to it if we had wings. But I was painfully aware that we had neither sails nor oars. We were close; about three miles of sea separated us from the island.

While we were drifting on the enormous sea, I thought that if we detected an island, our rescue would be immediate. However, that was not the case. I was worried about becoming disoriented and drifting out to sea again. So without hesitation, I stripped naked and dove into the sea. Although a little unsure, I thought I could swim and slowly push the boat to the island. From inside the boat, Hideo earnestly rowed with his hands spread out like a maple tree. Despite all of this effort, I could barely tell whether the boat was moving or not? Progress was slow, but our hard work paid off. It took half a day, but we reached the island. Crossing just three miles on the waves at a plodding speed took over six hours. I was drained to the edge of death.

After hauling the boat that guarded our fate for over ten days onto the shore, I concluded that it was mid May. Verdant trees and shrubs covered the entire island. There were fields and mountains as far as I could see. The area where we landed was a green field of native grasses. Red and white flowers whose names were unknown to me bloomed all around. Each time a southern breeze gently blew, an exquisite fragrance from the shore to the sea flowed over us. We were at the border of the playground of supernatural beings. We had been dropped from an extreme predicament into much easier circumstances. For the first time, I suspected we may be in a dream. My tension eased, but fatigue and hunger returned.

I scanned the island wondering if there was anything to eat. As expected, I saw a tract of coconut palms and banana trees on a small hill about a fifth of a mile away. Beautiful ripe fruits hung from just broken branches.

We ran up the hill as if we had wings. We didn't wonder whether something was edible or not, we just ate until our bellies were full. The next problem was what kind of island had we landed on? Looking out, the island seemed immense, but where on earth was it? Was it far off in the east? Maybe, we had landed on an island in the Borneo archipelago?

I concluded from my analysis of the climate and the types of vegetation that we were close to the coast of Africa. However, no amount of speculation would reveal the truth to me. A major problem was whether this island was uninhabited? In either case, I had to be prepared. I had to know if good people inhabited the island or if I would encounter the haunts of fearsome savages. Either way, I had to have a plan for a fast exit. I concluded that an exploration of the island was necessary. So I took the boy's hand and we set off.

A tour of the island would reveal its size. There may be danger along the way, but I wasn't sure. I also knew nothing about the origin of this island. I intended to walk until dusk as far as my legs could carry me; that was better than spending a miserable night of not knowing.

First, I had to decide which direction to take. To get a better view, we passed through the grove and climbed to the top of a hill. To the north was the ocean we had come from. I couldn't tell what was off in the distance. Our abandoned boat swayed gently on the waves on the sea coast we were overlooking. A flock of curious sea birds had gathered and were flying around it. The three directions of east, west, and south of the island were verdant forests as far as I could see. A few scattered mountains as well as valleys were visible. And a distant strip of silver that appeared and disappeared was a river.

Surveying the scene, I truly lost heart. Without a doubt, I was looking at a desert island. The entire island was covered with mountains, forests, and valleys. I couldn't decide which direction to take. Going deep into the mountains from here would invite danger. For the time being, I suspended any exploration of the island. As I turned to go back to the beach, Hideo said, "Hey, what's that sound?" He stopped and stared.

"You heard something?" I froze to listen carefully and heard echoes carried on the wind. I thought the island was uninhabited, but I heard echoes of a rhythmic clanging of iron against iron coming from far down in a valley.

I tilted my head to listen, "That's hammering!"

There shouldn't be a blacksmith on an isolated island like this. Was my mind playing tricks on me? No, it was not. I was already certain that the strange echoes in the silent sky were sounds of hammering. But I realized the source of those echoes was not nearby. It was quiet in all directions and I could distinctly hear something. It was coming from at least three or four miles away. More than what that sound was, who was there? I wondered were they people or evil spirits? We had to prepare for our expedition and slowly descended the hill.

At the bottom of the hill, I listened again. These sounds, whatever they were, seemed to be coming from beyond a large promontory on the southwest side of the island. I was determined to explore the island. This situation was eerie. I didn't know who was making those sounds nor what misfortune would arise along the way. I had to prepare for an emergency. I firmly moored the boat on the shore and tore up my white shirt to use as a sign to locate the boat in a glance. Now with a mission, I set off with the boy.

About half a mile along the shore we came to a rocky hill. After climbing over this hill, the seascape was no longer visible, and the sounds of the waves gradually receded. The boy seemed exhausted, so I lifted him onto my shoulders and pressed on. Although a quiet place, the sound of my footsteps were so noisy, we couldn't even chat. Of course, there were no roads, and I had to push my way through bamboo. Fallen leaves had accumulated for hundreds or thousands of years and resembled a small mountain. In addition, bits of a yellow resin particular to the southern hemisphere clumped the leaves together. In this peculiar forest, the trunks of the several hundred trees were arranged in a regular grid, like the poles of a tent. After walking for about a mile and a half, we came to the edge of a spring gushing out dazzling waters. The colors of the plants in this area were enchanting. It looked like a good place to sit and rest. It was close to five o'clock in the afternoon, but the mysterious echoes were near at last.

Hideo discovered gorgeous small fish in the spring. While he eagerly followed the fish, I lay down in the shade of a curious large tree and soon dozed off. When I was somewhere between dreams and reality and enveloped in various thoughts, the boy jumped back to my knees and shook my shoulders to awaken me.

"Oh no! Uncle, a ferocious beast...."

"A ferocious beast!" I was jolted out of my dreams.

When I looked where the boy was pointing, something was terribly wrong! From the yellow resin forest we had passed through earlier, a beast charged into view.

"It's a gorilla!" I shouted. The hairs on my arms stood up.

In this world, no animal is as ferocious as a lion, as vicious as a wolf, nor as terrifying as a gorilla. Even a glimpse of that vicious face peering out through the bars of an iron cage sends shivers through you. I was overwhelmed by that face rushing through this forest to attack us. For a second, I thought about escape, but what would be the result? When I was prepared to die, the gorilla was almost upon us. He was close to seven feet tall. His silvery fur stiffened. He bared his sharp fangs and towered over us. He may have inhabited this forest for one hundred or so years.

The nature of the savage ape is to not rush into a fight. He bares his teeth and sneers in anger. As I was preparing myself, he let out a loud growl that sent shivers down my spine, like I had been doused with freezing water. What could I do? I shielded the boy behind me and glared into the gorilla's eyes. While a wild animal is under the penetrating gaze of a man, no harm will come. But his gaze will gradually weaken, and before long, the man is caught off guard, and in a breath, the beast leaps. Therefore, I am prepared to be eaten, but if I am to die, I will not go easily. If the hairy beast let his guard down for a moment as I stared at him, I would inflict some pain by making a preemptive leap. The gorilla also glaring fiercely sprinted toward me. At the juncture of a narrow escape from death, an unexpected gunshot rang out, closely followed by another. The gorilla hit by unforeseen bullets leaped up as if kicking the ball in a game of *kemari*. Startled, we both turned around. No more than two hundred yards away two men emerged from the forest.

Surprised and overjoyed, both the boy and I shouted, "They're Japanese! They're Japanese!"

Was this a dream? The two men who emerged were undeniably Japanese. One man was a muscular sailor dressed in black and wearing a long sword across his hip. He stared sternly at us. The other man was dressed in the majestic uniform of a naval officer in the Imperial Navy and was holding the handle of a double-barreled gun. When he turned to look at the sailor, the sailor energetically ran five or six steps closer. As we watched, the gorilla flicked aside the two bullets that hit him and roared as he rushed forward like a wildly galloping horse. He sprang above the sailor's head at lightning speed. As we watched, the sailor deftly ducked and sliced the gorilla's shoulder in an unseen overarm stroke. When the incensed gorilla grabbed the sword with both hands, the irritated sailor slammed his foot into the gorilla's chest. During this grand struggle, the calm naval officer quietly approached. He appeared to be pointing the gun's muzzle at the gorilla's heart and immediately took one shot. The seven-foot gorilla let out a cry of pain, vomited fresh blood and dropped to the ground.

The boy and I felt as though we were in a dream

watching a dream. The sailor resembled the guardian diety *Skanda* as he raced to us, then astride the animal he delivered the fatal blow. The naval officer calmly approached us. I can't describe my elation. However, when I saw his face, I felt an electrical shock surge through me and shouted, "You're Captain Sakuragi!"

Also surprised, the Captain studied my face.

"Oh, it's you," he said, and for a short time, said nothing more.

Captain Sakuragi! Does that name jog your memory? When I left the Port of Naples, he was the leading character in that cryptic article in the old newspaper that had grabbed my attention. By then, the Captain had kept the secret for a year and a half and boarded a mysterious sailing ship one night with the thirty-seven sailors under his command and left Japan. I could never have imagined encountering this man on this desert island. Absolutely unbelievable! I wandered in a fog for a time.

12

THE NAVY HOUSE

A **few moments later,** Captain Sakuragi said, as he appraised us, "This is truly amazing...your landing on this isolated island."

"This desert island is far off in the southern end of the Indian Ocean. The nearest island in the Madagascar archipelago is over one thousand miles away, and the Asian and European continents are perhaps several thousand miles away. For someone to land on this island is extraordinary," he said, looking a little suspicious.

"Yes it is," I offered. Naturally, in that kind of situation, any suspicion would not be openly stated. But when I traced the events from the sinking of the ship to drifting to this island, the Captain seemed to be convinced for the first time.

"I imagined something like that had happened. You have faced true adversity," he said, his eyes fixed on the bullet-punctured corpse of the gorilla.

"Actually, I decided earlier to go hunting with this crewman. Fortunately, we were able to rescue you," he said looking at the sky.

"I wish to hear more details, but it's getting dark and the gorilla's nest is probably nearby, so we should return home," he said as he raised the barrel of his gun. As I was about to say something, Hideo briefly spoke. The Captain turned his commanding gaze to the boy.

"What a cute child," he said while gently patting the boy's cheek. He looked back at the intrepid sailor and said, "Seaman Takemura. Take care of this little fellow."

Seaman Takemura promptly scooped up the boy.

"Oh, what a cute guy. You'll ride on my shoulders," he said and immediately took off running. Captain Sakuragi lived about a mile away. I suddenly realized that that place may have been the source of the earlier echoes of iron. As we walked, the Captain peppered me with a variety of questions. However, I did not ask a word about the Captain's current situation. There was no pressing need to ask anything. I thought it would be rude to make rash inquiries into the secrets of the solemn Captain. However, propelled by the old newspaper article from many nights ago, the audible echoes of iron, which we could still hear, hazy thoughts were fostered in my mind about the presence of the Captain on this desert island outside of our fleeting world. Had Captain Sakuragi planned to hide away on this island to embark on the discovery of a major military invention? Perhaps, you, the reader, had also imagined this?

After walking about half a mile from the site of our clash with the gorilla, we saw the ocean again. We passed over two hills, a clear stream, and through a dim, deep forest to a place where our field of vision expanded. From there, we could see the Captain's house built on a cliff rising more than several hundred feet above the sea surface. The house faced the expanse of the Indian Ocean. Behind it was a beautiful grove of coconut palms. Naturally, being on an isolated island, the building wasn't particularly attractive, but it was a fairly large house with a shingled roof. *The Navy House* was inscribed in bold strokes at the entrance. The thirty-seven sailors under his command probably lived in the line of some number of long, misshapen rooms that I could see. Three more presentable rooms were on the second floor. A white curtain fluttering in the window of one room was surely the Captain's sitting room. As we approached the house, Seaman Takemura with Hideo on his shoulders was running at full speed, cheerfully shouting, "Oy, Seamen! Fall in! The Captain's back with a rare guest and this cute guy. Hurry! Come greet them!"

In response to his call, a group of sailors who remained in the house came flying out of the same room. These strapping men, who looked like they had just beat back the devil, formed a line in front of the house and saluted. Seaman Takemura seemed to be a leader among his fellow sailors. The group of valiant sailors threw their hats up high and yelled, "*Banzai!*" They were probably celebrating our safe landing on this island as friends of the venerated Captain Sakuragi. The Captain looked at them and revealed a small smile.

"Thank you all so much," I blurted out, unable to hold back my tears of joy. The innocent Hideo's eyes widened, and he started dancing on Seaman Takemura's shoulder. The cheery group of sailors encircled them.

"Hey, he's cute...Let me take care of him...No me," they clamored.

Captain Sakuragi raised his right hand and said, "Settle down men. The child is exhausted.

"Hurry and prepare a guest room. Clean up Room No. 2, the extra reading room on the second floor."

After giving his orders, the Captain took Hideo off of

Seaman Takemura's shoulder, turned to me and said, "First, come with me to my quarters."

He took us to the room at the southern end of the second floor. The room was about fifteen square feet. A circular table stood in the center. On the table were a globe of the world and some kind of compass. Maps of the world's nations hung without even the tiniest gap between them on all four walls. Clearly, I was looking at the room of a naval officer. In this room, the Captain gave us a cordial welcome. The coffee brought by the sailors wet my throat. I smoked to satisfaction the cigar I had craved ever since we were set adrift. Although a hideous sight, I savored the sweet candies made by the cook. After about fifteen minutes had passed, it was 6 pm. The sky of that long day in May resembled the sun setting behind Nishiyama.

At that moment, the Captain quietly stood, turned to me, and said, "I have duties to attend to. Please excuse me. You two should rest. I will return a little after eight, and we will dine together," then he left.

Later, the always cheerful Seaman Takemura came. With a kindness inconsistent with his rough appearance, he had arranged for replacements for our tattered clothes, which had been dunked into the sea and burned in the sun, ordered a sailor to mend Hideo's little flannel sailor suit, and arranged baths for us. A room had been prepared as the Captain had ordered, and he took us there. After many days, we could lie down on beds.

For the first time, Hideo and I looked at each other and rejoiced in our unforeseen good luck and grateful for the kind reception by the Captain and his crew. I've told you many things, but the accumulated fatigue from the past dozen or so days put both of us into a deep sleep.

13

TWINKLING STARLIGHT

I had no idea how long we slept, but I was startled awake by a loud voice saying, "Sir, it's already dark, and the Captain has kept you waiting, but at last it's dinner time. Namizo, the cook, burnt the roasted bird, and the fried eggs are black and white."

When I regained my senses, the sun had set. I gazed out the glass window at the twinkling starlight bouncing off the ocean's surface. I had been awakened by the cheery Seaman Takemura. Clinging to his right hand was a grinning Hideo.

"Uncle, I already washed my face," he said, looking up at my grumpy morning face.

Not wanting to look like a sleepyhead to the boy, I sprang up and splashed my face with spring water. The Seaman guided us to a room, there, Captain Sakuragi was sitting at one end of the dining table absorbed in conversation with a few high-ranking sailors. When he spied us, he smiled and said, "Excuse me for having Takemura disturb your peaceful slumber," and ordered a sailor to bring two chairs. At the other end of the table, Seaman Takemura and three other sailors stood at attention. At our end, the Captain and I were seated shoulder to shoulder with Hideo slipped in between, and we soon began our meal. A brilliant light shone from the lamp. The rustic-looking but kindhearted seamen had taken the time to skillfully arrange the emerald flowers of the Chinese white olive on a wall into the word *Welcome*.

The Captain apologized for being unable to provide suitable food for the occasion because of the island's isolation. However, through the great efforts of the cook, we were able to enjoy delicious pan-baked eggs of a soft-shell turtle, oysters boiled in a salted broth, and a roasted bird having a delicate flavor. The bird, commonly known as an *Iwa* duck, appeared to be from the large flock of wild ducks native to this island. But I felt one hundred times happier than if I had been served the world's most coveted delicacy at the world's premiere hotel.

As we began to enjoy tea after dinner, Captain Sakuragi asked first, but was soon joined by our other dinner companions wanting a detailed account about what brought us to this island. I took a sip of my coffee and proceeded to leisurely recount my tale. First, I described my objective of traveling the world. I told them about leaving the Port of Yokohama and first crossing over to America and my travels in various European countries. I told them about my unexpected encounter with Hamajima Takebumi, my old friend from school and now the owner of a foreign mercantile house, at the Port of Naples in Italy; the mysterious connection to his wife, Harue, and their treasured son, Hideo, who I hadn't met yet, and our return to Japan together on the same ship, the *Crescent Moon*; and before we left the port, the earnest plea from the superstitious old Italian woman, Annie, to not leave on that night, the Devil's Hour on the Day of the Devil.

I described every event, leaving nothing out, until we drifted onto this island, the baffling incident of the binoculars, our trials and tribulations on the Indian Ocean from the beginning to the end, the praiseworthy behavior of Harue, only Harue going missing despite all three of us jumping together into the sea from the deck of the *Crescent Moon*, and our entire ordeal while we were adrift. My rapt audience experienced emotions from surprise to sadness. As he listened with his eyes wide open, Seaman Takemura stood like a wooden statue, barely breathing, as did the others.

When I finished, Captain Sakuragi raised his head and spoke, "Your journey sounds like fiction."

He studied my face for a short time. As I spoke, he was particularly moved by the laudable actions of Harue. Captain Sakuragi was close to Harue's elder brother, Captain Matsushima, more than some brothers are to each other, and often saw him while in Japan. During those visits, he often saw his younger sister, the young maiden Harue. Upon hearing about that beautiful woman's disappearance into the waves of the Indian Ocean, the mournful Captain was incredulous and could think of nothing else.

"Nevertheless, I've always held a firm belief in some unforeseen power in heaven. A beautiful woman in body and spirit often receives extraordinary help even in the face of death."

As he spoke, my thoughts briefly returned to the night my dear mother died, and I patted the head of the grieving Hideo.

"I also want to believe that Harue was rescued unharmed. This may be a strange thing to say, but people possess a type of empathy. For a person like me separated by distance and time, you will believe 'that person is still safe' without proof of death. Despite hearing that Harue was swallowed by the waves, I refuse to believe she met an unhappy end. She may have been unexpectedly rescued and returned home to Naples, and is now distressed over your fates." He paused and patted the back of Hideo's lowered head.

"The behavior of the pirate ship was despicable. In time, that godless ship will be smashed to smithereens."

His bright eyes radiated an awe-inspiring light. Hearing this, Hideo jumped up and said, "That's right. If my uncles in the Navy destroy the pirate ship, I will fight the enemy admiral."

"That's the spirit of a true Japanese boy!" exclaimed Seaman Takemura who had been as mute as a wooden statue.

"When that moment comes, Takemura Shinpachiro will lead the advance guard," he said repeatedly banging the table. The plates jumped, and knives fell to the floor. Like me, the seamen laughed at the talk of the Devil's Hour on the Day of the Devil. Only Captain Sakuragi did not laugh. Naturally, no one believes such inauspicious things, but the old woman Annie may have somehow known that a pirate ship had targeted the *Crescent Moon*.

Although this doesn't entirely explain our situation, she had to endure my indifferent face to the disaster about to befall her master's house. If I had believed her ominous story, our departure that night may have been stopped. Of course, if I had tried to listen, I would have had difficulty understanding. Our conversation often touched on the affair of the pirate ship, the *Sea Snake*.

According to the Captain, there had been rumors about a pirate island and secret agreements between pirates and some powerful nation. These were mostly open secrets among seamen well-versed in matters of the sea.

The seamen all agreed that those fiends had to be eliminated. The shameful behavior of the entire crew, beginning with the captain, at the brink of the *Crescent Moon*'s sinking surprised and enraged my listeners. The eyes of the impetuous Seaman Takemura blazed.

"What scum!" he shouted, "That cowardly captain running away is a crime. He's probably dead, swallowed by the waves. But if, by chance, he survived, I, Takemura Shinpachiro, will not accept that...he will be made an example to the world...Let me at him!"

The Captain laughed, the sailors slapped his arms. Hideo and I looked at each other with delight.

Without my noticing, night had fallen as I told the story. When my tale of misfortune was over, Captain Sakuragi with a slightly different expression looked at me.

"From your story, I now understand the circumstances of your drifting to this island, but what are you intent on doing now?"

What am I intent on doing? We had drifted to this desert island. My thoughts were between wanting to return home, even if that was nearly impossible, and preparing to stay on this island with the Captain and his crew until I could return. Naturally, I ached to return home to Japan as soon as possible, but considering the current situation, I couldn't say something so selfish to this man. I simply replied, "We leave our fates to heaven and to you, Captain."

The Captain nodded and said, "In that case, you'll have to remain on this island for some time."

I nodded.

The Captain continued, "In truth, there's no other option. Of course, if you were determined to leave your fate to heaven and cross the waves of the Indian Ocean in a small boat again to return to Japan, I would never wish such injustice on you. Since you can't possibly leave this island today or tomorrow by some other means, for the time being, your only choice is to remain on this desert island with our crew."

"I am prepared for that," I responded, "We are useless. I'm only concerned about the trouble we are causing you."

The Captain interrupted, "No, no. To the contrary, I feel terrible about making you long for home from this far off island thousands of miles across the sea."

"Well, if the *Bay of Waves* were sound...," he said looking at Seaman Takemura. The *Bay of Waves* was the large sailing ship first mentioned in that old newspaper and had transported the Captain and his crew to this island. For some reason, this ship was not near this shore. When I peered out the window, I only saw a few lonely small boats floating on the ocean waves reflecting the starlight, but no ship.

With arms folded, Seaman Takemura said to the boy, "Well, an unfortunate event occurred. We would have been safe if we had the *Bay of Waves*. I would skillfully seize the tiller and take you straight to Japan. But on the night of the last big storm, it was washed ashore and damaged. So now, it's useless."

"But this island's lotsa fun. There are tons of fish to catch. And I can hunt lions, too. Right now, I don't wanna go home."

While smiling wryly, the Captain only asked me, "Who would want to live forever on an isolated island like this?"

He declared with dignity, "However, everything is heaven's will. But don't despair. When will we be joyous and look down on the tops of the cotton roses...I'm sure that time will be three years from now." He looked toward the shore where the ocean was breaking against the head sea rocks.

14

THE UNDERSEA SHIPYARD

The following morning, when Hideo and I awoke at eight, Captain Sakuragi had already set off with a group of sailors, including Seaman Takemura, to some unknown destination. The cook brought our breakfast and informed us the Captain would not be joining us that morning. He said, "The Captain has duties to attend to this morning, but forgot to mention one important thing last night. Because you were still asleep when he left this morning, he left me to warn you. Within a mile and a half of here, you are free to roam anywhere, but many dangers, like poisonous snakes, which you should never step on, lurk beyond that boundary. The Captain will return tonight and see you then."

The boy and I were drained by our ordeal over the last two weeks and had no interest in hiking. Nevertheless, this warning made us more wary. After breakfast, my plan was to write in my diary. We would spend the day at the shore gazing at the immense sea from the rocks, knocking a few of the beautiful fruits off the trees in the coconut palm grove behind the house to the ground, and fishing for sea turtles near the rocky coast pointed out by a sailor who had remained behind.

After dusk when they returned, both Captain Sakuragi and Seaman Takemura were exhausted. But one look at our faces appearing much healthier than yesterday after a long day of relaxation brought forth gales of laughter. We spent that evening engaged in pleasant conversations covering many topics until midnight.

I rose around six the next morning, I believe just before the Captain went out. A little after the Captain left, the boy and I were looking out a window on the second floor at the morning fog blanketing the shore. About a mile and a half past our home was a bay where the white choppy sea smashed against the rocks. The rocks in the bay zigzagged like a folding screen and formed into a natural crucible. We spied the Captain's back in that area.

"Hey, my Navy Uncle is hiding behind those rocks," said Hideo who looked at me perplexed. I said nothing, but carefully studied that area. For a short time, I heard the clanging echoes of iron from yesterday and the day before coming from the mysterious shadows of the rocks.

Seaman Takemura unexpectedly returned home alone a little after ten that morning.

"Now, we're off to hunt down a lion," said the brave man. I hesitated, a bit distressed by this undertaking. With this energetic man as my guide on a trek around this island of mountains, rivers, valleys, thick forests, and a rocky coasts with craggy rocks jutting out like swords, I was worn ragged. In order to avoid the dangers of wild animals and poisonous snakes during our trek, a fierce dog under the command of Seaman Takemura prowled in front or behind us.

The dog's name was Lightning. He was Captain Sakuragi's prized dog because he was a sturdy, large animal, the size of a calf, with jet black fur and a neatly curled tail. Hideo was fascinated by him and was constantly calling out, "Lightnin', Lightnin'." When the dog came, they would run around and before long were great friends. When Lightning returned in the evening, he played with the boy. Before we knew it, he would bound upstairs, and Seaman Takemura had to chase him out. Hideo chucked the delicious steak from his supper out the window to the dog. Before long, Hideo's best friend was Lightning, so naturally he no longer was only by my side. He went out early in the morning astride Lightning's back and hugging his neck to play along the shore in the blue waves and white sands.

I remained alone, shut up in my room. That morning, the Captain asked me to translate a book on navigation that he started to translated long ago in his spare time. That's how I would spend the day. The remaining twenty percent of the book was tedious and I tackled it reluctantly. Around dusk when I finished, the Captain and his band of sailors had already returned along the shore.

Both last night and the night before, I opened the room window after finishing supper and engaged in various conversations while taking in the cool air from the sea. When I placed a chair near the fluttering white curtain as usual, Captain Sakuragi was looking at me. He said, "I have something I wish to talk to you about later tonight."

What could it be? When my demeanor suddenly changed, the Captain threw his cigar butt out the window and quietly spoke. He began, "Yanagawa, I have been thinking about this ever since we unexpectedly saved you from disaster while passing through that forest covered in that milky yellowish resin. The chance of anyone coming to this isolated island is slim to none, pure chance. And seeing a face from home seems like guidance from heaven. For the next few years, our fates will be to live in the same place and look on the same moon. What could be the connection?

"I have a secret. This secret is known to only me, my thirty-seven trusted sailors, and certain government officials in the Imperial Navy. This secret has never been divulged to anyone else. As you will live here over many months in this situation, from time to time, you will see things."

He slowly raised his eyes and said, "And you've probably wondered why I came to this island and what is going on here?"

I gulped and responded, "I do have some vague notions."

The Captain nodded, "This secret is truly my life. Do you remember a few years ago when I recited my unusual poem on the deck of the steamship? By comparing the increase in the naval power of European nations and the current situation in our country, today, our nation ranks behind many of them in the large number of warships and in the manufacture of diverse weapons due to wealth and advances in mechanical engineering. I have little hope that we will maintain and advance absolute peace in the East and seize great power in diplomacy. We must garner the determination to leapfrog Europe and the United States.

"Namely, we will develop an earthshaking military invention. This invention is for our country alone. It will be an important secret military weapon and must absolutely not be seen abroad. We will be here until Europe and America can no longer be impertinent to Japan. You shouted with delight at the call for the need to invent an important weapon that will leave the world in awe. That too was a wish buried deep in my heart.

"As the result of painstaking work over several years, on November 30 of last year, I gathered a large quantity of materials and my trusted crew of thirty seven on a large sailing ship and left Japan far behind. Concealing myself on this desert island was all planned in advance, and we embarked on the development of this major military invention. Although unworthy, I am devoting all my strength to begin the production of a powerful weapon unheard of in previous generations for our nation's Imperial Navy."

Just as I had suspected! My heart jumped. The Captain continued, "There were probably rumors flying around some circles in Japan, and you probably had a few ideas. In order to keep others from finding out until some kind of invention was completed, I hid myself here on this isolated island to maintain complete secrecy from the military spies of foreign nations and from the designs of some very selfish people. Its manufacture is also top secret."

More forcefully, he added, "But Yanagawa, you have mysteriously joined our company by an act of heaven. Considering the situation from here on, I have faith in you. If you have given your word of honor, today, I trust in the wisdom in disclosing this important secret to you."

"Tell me an important secret?" I asked as I rose from my chair.

In a composed voice, the Captain said, "I trust you. If you promise to keep this secret forever as my confidant, you must make a solemn vow three times to heaven."

When I vowed without hesitation, the Captain quickly rose and grabbed my hand.

"The vow was a formality. You with your deep love of

country wouldn't accidentally leak this secret to some worthless outsider."

"I give my word. My lips are sealed." I was steadfast.

The Captain smiled as he looked at me. The secret is an actual object. This night ended with that simple oath. Tomorrow, the details will be revealed in the form of an actual object at a hidden location. I lay in my bed that night, but thoughts kept popping up and I couldn't fall asleep until late in the night. People are willful creatures. Despite not being able to sleep until midnight, the next morning, I rose while it was still dark. Around half past five, Captain Sakuragi accompanied by Seaman Takemura knocked on my door. We were to go to the secret location.

We left the house and went north along the shore cloaked by a thick morning mist. Seaman Takemura gave commands to the fierce dog, Lightning. They were always ahead of us by ten steps. The Captain and I walked side by side, but did not speak. What could this secret invention be? If it's a powerful weapon, it may be a kind of bomb having extraordinary explosive force, or the invention of a giant gun having phenomenal power. No, it's probably a more powerful invention as the Captain said. As I was dreaming up various possibilities, we arrived.

We were near the sheer cliffs in the bay where I glimpsed the Captain's back early yesterday morning. My first impression of the area was the peculiar shapes of the rocks, which resembled a folding screen. From a distance, they looked like isolated slabs, but after climbing above them and looking down, they were many identically shaped, overlapping rock slabs everywhere resembling the roof of an immense palace in ancient Rome. Without a doubt, below us was a huge cave. Despite surging waves breaking on all sides, the interior of the cave was tranquil and each step we took echoed. Just twenty yards beyond the sheer rocks was a single iron gate in the center of a massive rock rising in the front like a wall. In front of the iron gate stood an armed sailor, he acknowledged the Captain with a salute. On closer examination, I noticed an inscription above the iron gate, *The Secret Shipyard*.

15

THE LIGHTNING SHIP

Seaman Takemura grabbed a large key on the lanyard hanging from his waist and opened the door in the iron gate. Captain Sakuragi turned to me and said, "This is the entrance to the secret location." It seemed like no one had begun work yet. I didn't hear the usual echoes of hammering iron. The interior was eerily silent. I followed the Captain and the Seaman through the iron gate. There wasn't much room so I had to crouch down for the first ten steps. Directly ahead of us was a steep stairway carved into the rock.

It was pitch black at the foot of the stairs. The desolate path appeared to be a tunnel. Seaman Takemura switched on a lantern to light our way. We turned right then left and walked about 140 or 150 yards to where the rock separated, the front from the back, to form a ravine. The tide flowed in and out of the cave like an arrow. We crossed the bridge spanning the ravine to another iron door. Again, Seaman Takemura pushed the door open. We were instantly flooded with, what was no doubt, sunlight. Beyond the door was brightly lit. Just as Seaman Takemura quenched the light from the lantern, Captain Sakuragi simply said, "This is it."

I followed him through the iron gate into a colossal cave and found myself surrounded on all sides by rocks that looked chiseled. At the top, a huge fissure opened up like a skylight to bathe the interior of the cave with sunlight. When I stopped to listen, I could hear thundering waves coming from somewhere. The source seemed to be outside the sheer walls. I was probably several dozen feet down on the sea floor listening to the turbulent waves.

Naturally, the scene was a curiosity. I was at the frontier of humanity and suspected I had been transported to some otherworldly place. As I calmed down and looked around, the site resembled a small shipyard. The interior of the huge cave was divided into several sections. Of course, the site had a dock and a derrick. There was a bloomery with a furnace and a hammer. A foundry was equipped with a molding machine and a crushing roller. The lathe had a vertical cutter, a horizontal cutter, a whetting machine, and a punch machine. The boiler provided a hydraulic riveting machine. The iron working room was equipped with a bending machine and a shearing machine.

Stacked near the circular and band saws were square bars and iron materials, as well as, elaborate machinery like an air pressing pump and an electric power generator, and silver solder, pewter, tar rope, manila rope, twine, twisted yarn, emery cloth, black lead, volatile oils, refined oil, radium paint, rust-colored paint, copper sheets, iron sheets, steel plates, zinc cakes, cutter backer boards, ebonite boards, glass plates, glass pipes, thick glass for ship windows, spiral tack, steel rivets, brass rivets, asbestos packing, and elastic packing.

How could all of these preparations been made on this isolated island? It appeared that two years ago, all of these machines and materials had been loaded onto the large sailing ship *Bay of Waves* and transported to this island. Everything was arranged in its proper place. There were obvious signs that the machinery had already been used many times.

The center of the mysterious shipyard caught my eye. There the shape of the uneven rocks formed a natural shipbuilding berth, and an unusual-looking hull was under construction.

"This is my secret construction of the Undersea Warship," said Captain Sakuragi as he slowly raised his right hand and pointed to the ship's hull. My heart pounded as I studied every inch of the ship's body. It was fantastic. A ship so mysterious and so sturdy was probably a warship. When I glimpsed its outer form, I was struck by the exquisite workmanship. Led by the Captain, we entered the half-completed Undersea Warship that has taken most of two years to achieve. I studied the various structures of the ship: the upper deck, the lower deck, the water way, the wing passage, the double bottom, and the ribs. I could only marvel at human ingenuity as he explained the infinite variety of machines and was unable to stifle my shouts of admiration.

Construction of this phenomenal undersea warship continued through the night under the supervision of Captain Sakuragi in this secret shipyard hidden in this cave. The addition of this exceptional warship some day to the military vessels of the Empire of Japan upon its successful completion will resonate through the world's naval forces. I assert that this ship flying the Rising Sun flag will take its place among the fleets of the world's great powers, fierce as an eagle and brave as a lion, and perhaps dominate them.

Dear Reader, I ache to explain every detail about the

construction of this astonishing and awe-inspiring Undersea Warship, unfortunately, these are Captain Sakuragi's important secrets. Without violating this secrecy, I can tell you that the Undersea Warship is 130 feet 6 inches long, and 22 feet 7 inches wide at the center cross-section. Its shape closely resembles the shape of the spear used by a South Indian savage to kill a giant elephant or slay a ferocious tiger in a single blow. Both ends of the ship are formed into unusually sharp angles. The distinctive feature of a sharp angle is critical for speed.

An elliptical watch tower was positioned in the upper bow of the ship with only one signal mast on top of the tower. An automatic iron door was installed on one end. Naturally, this door closed when the ship was on the verge of submerging and instantly reopened upon resurfacing.

The entire ship was built from metal. Not just the watch tower and the upper deck, the helm, the missile room, the crew's quarters were all protected by sturdy armor. This armor was some new type of armor plating having a flexibility and a resistant power surpassing that of several sheets of the current steel plates or nickel plates processed by the Harvey method. The result of the painstaking work of Captain Sakuragi over many months was the development of six metal alloys believed to possess sufficient resistance to any state-of-the-art missile or torpedo. This new alloy armor plate covered every critical part of the Undersea Warship.

I described the exterior of this ship, but not the methods that enable the Undersea Warship to instantly sink an enemy ship. This will be accomplished by the actions of two different weapons. I don't completely understand them because they are now under construction. However, one mystifying weapon is called the Enemy Ship

Striker, an extremely strong ram installed at the front of the ship.

This ram is quite different from the conventional ones mounted on armored ships or cruisers. Its shape resembled a pointed funnel and projected at least seventeen feet from the front of the ship. By the actions of an internal engine, the sharp funnel-shaped ram rotates like a winch at a speed of 300 revolutions per second. Any warship not equipped with at least 14.5 inches of armor will be shredded when touched by the ram. However, this funnel-shaped ram is not a remarkable weapon for the Undersea Battleship. More surprising is the new Parallel Rotating Torpedo Gun installed on both sides of the ship.

With so many exquisite wonders in the structure of the torpedo gun, I was unable to understand the explanation without detailed drawings. First, there is a polished mirror in the secret room equipped with the firing tubes. The circumstances on the sea bottom and on the surface can be observed by the actions of electrical currents and the actions of 230 reflecting mirrors. An automatic illumination device is used to determine the tide speed and set the direction of the wave motion. If the naval battle has already begun, this ship will run like an electric light below the waves.

While standing there and observing the situations on the surface and the bottom of the sea shown in the polished mirror, the torpedo sighting board is simply operated during the day, but during night warfare, an ignition electric lock is pulled to radiate intense white- and green-colored electric lights. By setting the sight and turning the rotating wheel, electric bells ring instantly and the firing frame moves to fire seventy-eight fish-shaped torpedoes like rain or hail in one minute.

The fish-shaped torpedoes are just two feet three inches

long with a maximum diameter just over three inches. Although just one seventh the size of the fish-shaped Holland torpedo often used in naval warfare today, an air-flask, a buoyancy chamber, and a tail are all neatly arranged inside. The detonation powder, which takes up most of the warhead, is equivalent to the 175 kilograms of guncotton in the warhead of a conventional fish-shaped torpedo. Able to travel an effective distance of 1,400 yards at a speed of forty-one knots, trapped inside the thundering sounds of gunfire and gunpowder smoke in naval warfare, you could look through the polished mirror and see the torpedo skimming the surface kicking up waves like a submarine dragon or a killer whale. At lightning speed, a turn of the firing slewing ring would smash starboard torpedoes into the starboard side and send the enemy ship to the bottom or smash port side torpedoes into the enemy ship if its port side was exposed.

Earlier, I sketched the configuration of the new torpedo firing tube and its extraordinary operation, but I was able to tour the entire Undersea Warship. She was divided into about a dozen compartments from the central weapons room, including a nautical chart room, a control room, and a searchlight room. In particular, the diving station and the engine room were the most important parts, but I cannot say one word about them in order to keep my vow.

I'll divulge just a little more. The power for controlling the operation of the multitude of engines of this ship is neither the familiar steam power nor electrical power. It is a type of chemical action previously unknown in this century. The result of Captain Sakuragi's painstaking work over many months was the discovery of a compound of secret amounts of twelve, also secret, chemicals possessing an action more than thirty times stronger than ordinary electrical power. This discovery was applied to all of the engines on this ship. The ship's advance, the rotation of the funnel-shaped ram, and the operation of the new torpedo gun are all controlled by this secret energy.

Dear Reader, You may have sketched in your mind the construction and the amazing fighting strength of the vessel suggested by the above. Not to brag, but this mysterious Undersea Warship is a submarine that can compete with the improvements and advances made by the navies of the world. Although she is definitely a type of submarine, I am not satisfied with simply calling this military vessel a submarine, because it seems like today's inventors in Europe and America boast of having invented a novel submarine every year. Usually, all they accomplished were improvements to the water ballasts, the horizontal rudder, or the vertical rudder, or made a few trivial improvements to the exhaust pump or the diving machinery.

The power is not based on oil, electrical power is used. The ship's shape resembles a cigar that twists into a screw propeller blade. These examples only mimic the creations of inventors like Seeberger and Edison. Although a submarine does truly hide under the sea, typically, few of the earlier submarines rarely dove to depths below six feet because of the pressure of the seawater and the lack of air. And not one can stay submerged longer than an hour. Even in the first-class submarine in the Ciel Bleu Shipyard in France, known as the fastest of this century, satisfactory operation cannot be achieved because of these two defects. If the submarine managed to get close to the enemy ship, she would often attack with rapid-fire guns. This cannot be compared to Captain Sakuragi's unprecedented Undersea Warship.

This new Undersea Warship can dive to depths from thirty feet to fifty feet by the operation of automatic diving machinery provided in the bottom of the ship. By the operation of elaborate machinery installed at the stern of the ship that does not depend on an ordinary air reservoir or air compression pump, air passes through several hundred small, medium, and large zinc pipes and copper pipes that project into the sea from both sides of the ship to be reduced into hydrogen and oxygen by seawater. Air is guided in pipes above and below by a machine resembling a piston. Fresh air is sucked into the ship from one huge pipe as steam. Because bad molecules in the ship are completely exhausted to the outside, a lack of air is never felt inside. The ship can remain submerged as long as needed, be it ten hours or twenty hours.

The average speed is 56 knots, and the maximum is 107 knots. These astonishing speeds are, without a doubt, due to the shape of the ship and a power several dozen times stronger than steam power and electrical power. Remember that the power is in the mysterious rotating operation of spiral propellers with six blades positioned on both sides of the stern.

Dear Reader, I will now stop writing about the structure of this secret Undersea Warship. When this military ship, which would have no difficulty making headlines in today's world and in a future world, leaves this dock some day, the world's navies will be struck with surprise and terror. If the world sees some kind of monster, this vessel will be the most terrifying monster on the face of the Earth and be forever etched in the memories of the navies of Europe and America.

I'm sure that once the Undersea Warship kicks up seething waves and appears and disappears at will, shells will rain down on one hundred squadrons and one thousand battleships unable to evade her actions. Anyone acquainted with military matters knows that even a few shots from a Gatling gun, the world's most powerful gun, or a Caquot gun can't hit an object fourteen feet below the ocean surface. Moreover, because this Undersea Warship can stay submerged at thirty feet to fifty feet for an unlimited time, a battleship with this ship in its sights will be unable to escape, like a sheep bewitched by a stone guardian in the Arabian Desert in the old stories, nor fight, nor do anything to the sea monster that is untouched by the full power of rapid-firing guns and Gatling guns.

When alerted to the presence of an enemy ship while preparing for battle, the Undersea Warship can be swift or slow. If the enemy ship lacks armor, the parallel torpedo guns will not be used. The funnel-shaped ram will turn like a capstan. If the enemy ship is protected by at least fourteen inches of armor, the Undersea Warship will charge beneath the seething waves like electric light, assess the enemy's situation reflected in the mirror, and fire seventy-eight fish-shaped torpedoes per minute from the starboard and port by turns of the firing slewing ring. Even a large fleet formed from thirty first-class battleships can be annihilated in a flash.

Oh! The Undersea Warship! The Undersea Warship! In order to add this astonishing and fearsome naval vessel to the fleet of our Imperial Japanese Navy, this top-secret construction is advancing under the command of Captain Sakuragi in this wondrous undersea ship yard on a desert island.

Dear Reader! Needless to say, the day this Undersea Warship is successfully completed and glides on the expanse of blue waves of the world's oceans with the flag of the Imperial Navy fluttering high above her stern, as you expect, her primary mission will be war and, of course, to engage in fierce battles.

Two hours later, I was again outside the ship. My tour

of the Undersea Warship guided by Captain Sakuragi and Seaman Takemura was over. Although I had inspected the entire shipyard in the cave, I suddenly saw the rocks in a corner of the cave spontaneously turn and form a gigantic hole where a sturdy iron door was installed. *Life of the Undersea Warship* was painted in yellow on its front.

"What's that?" I quietly asked the Captain.

He replied, "That is the warehouse for storing the twelve barrels of critical chemicals for powering the Undersea Warship. In fact, these barrels of chemicals are more appropriately called the *Life of the Undersea Warship*."

I had so many questions about those barrels, but it was just before eight and the sailors had already gathered near the ship and started work. Also, Hideo was alone at the house on the coast and probably lonely and impatiently waiting for my return. I said goodbye to the Captain and was ready to leave. But before I left the Secret Shipyard, I wanted to ask two questions, "What is the completion date of the Undersea Warship? And what will she be named?"

The Captain gently stroked his mustache and replied, "Well, if all goes well, the test run will take place two years and nine months from now, around February 11, Empire Day. We will leave this island and should be able to again see the tops of the cotton roses we miss."

As for the name, he said, "Actually, she will be called *Lightning*."

Lightning! *Lightning*! When I remarked how fitting a name it was, the Captain continued, "The name of this ship came from one of my favorite poems by Yamaoka Tesshu."

"A poem by Yamaoka Tesshu?"

I nodded and immediately understood.

"Do you mean the verse 'Lightning slashes the spring wind'?"[1]

"Yes," said the Captain smiling.

"Some day, when our Undersea Warship flies the flag of the Imperial Navy and stands among the fleet of one thousand ships, I only hope she will be swift and fierce."

When our conversation ended, I said goodbye to the Captain and followed Seaman Takemura back down the mysterious road and out of The Secret Shipyard.

---

1. Stickgrappler's Sojourn of Septillion Steps website. Assorted poems by Yamaoka Tesshu. http://www.stickgrappler.net/2013/03/assorted-poems-by-yamaoka-tesshu.html (accessed December 19, 2014)

16

ASAHI ISLAND

I left the Secret Shipyard and parted company with Seaman Takemura at the iron gate. I followed Lightning at a quick pace and was soon back at the house on the coast. Hideo was standing alone at the gate in the shade of the coconut trees. When he saw me, he came running.

"Hey, Uncle. I wondered what happened to you. When I got up, you were gone. And I couldn't find Lightning either," he said, looking a little upset.

"Oh, you poor guy," I said and hugged him. Of course, I left with Captain Sakuragi and his company early that morning before dawn while the boy was still peacefully dreaming. When he awoke, I wasn't there as usual and neither was his cherished Lightning. He probably was surprised and lonely. I unexpectedly felt pity for him as I tried to explain.

"You see, Hideo, I didn't want to upset you, but the places I went to this morning were very dangerous, a very dark trail and a treacherous bridge. These places were only for grown-ups like the Captain and me. I left without telling you because if a small person like you went, you would have been so scared you'd want to cry."

Staring at me in disbelief, he said, "I don't cry, even in scary places like that."

"You don't cry?! You sure are strong! But you couldn't go because it was dangerous. Before long you'll be big enough and the Captain will gladly let you come along. Well, Lightning came back, too. Why don't you two go to the beach and play like you always do." Hearing that instantly cheered up Hideo. Although he looked like he wanted to hear more about the dark trail and the dangerous bridge, Lightning with his ears flopping and tail wagging came running up to us and captured Hideo's interest.

"Lightning! Where were you? Let's race!" He hopped away from me, touched Lightning's collar, and took off running toward the crashing waves.

I went inside and shut myself in my room all day. I had planned to compile this fantastic tale and would begin today. When I had recorded everything up to about chapter 3. *A Mysterious Ship* of this book, dusk had fallen. Hideo and Lightning had returned dead tired after a day spent running around. With Hideo sitting on my lap as we watched night fall, Captain Sakuragi, Seaman Takemura, and the rest of the sailors had finished their day's work and were returning from The Secret Shipyard.

Although dinner was the same as usual, that evening's dinner was particularly enjoyable to me. The reason being until the day before, I sensed that something important was going on, and Captain Sakuragi had not told me the secret shut away in his heart, which made me a little uncomfortable. But now, I knew everything about the Secret Shipyard and the Undersea Warship, and the Captain, who I held in such high esteem, trusted me enough to reveal this important secret. I was ecstatic and grateful for his favor, but was troubled by how to repay him for his kindness.

By chance, I had drifted onto the shore of this desert island, lived in the Captain's house, and have been treated with unusual kindness by him, Seaman Takemura, and the other sailors. I detested standing idly by with nothing to do as they labored each day. I approached them because it was my duty to offer my services.

"Captain, I have become one of this island's inhabitants and cannot bear standing idly by as your crew works hard each day. I'll do anything, carry iron materials, stoke coal for the steam-powered machines until the Undersea Warship is finished. Anything would be fine. Don't hesitate to use me in any way you see fit," I implored, but the Captain merely nodded.

"What? No. Don't worry about that. You and Hideo are our guests on this island. Just eat, rest, and do as you please. Until the day *Lightning* is completed, I am not bothered a bit if you just enjoy your stay," he said smiling at me.

He continued, "An intricate plan was developed to construct the Undersea Warship. We are not short by one man, nor do we need one more. The schedule will be met by exactly thirty-three sailors working for several years. You and the boy can just enjoy yourselves."

In the Captain's heart, our drifting to this desert island was unexpected, and our pathetic fate for the next few years was to live like caged birds and dream in vain of the skies of home. But I couldn't stay silent.

"No, that's no good. If I'm not needed in the Secret Shipyard, I'll be a cook," I appealed. Seaman Takemura, who was seated at the other side of the dining table and had been watching me in silence, suddenly poked out his head.

"Oh, I got a great job," he said in his usual frantic tone.

"You wanna be a cook? You can do that worthless job?" he said and looked at Captain Sakuragi, "Captain, this is an opportunity. How about asking him to build a monument tower on the island?"

The Captain clapped his hands together and said looking at me, "That's it! I was just thinking about that."

"If you really want to do something...," the Captain spoke with deliberation.

As I've told you, this desert island has never appeared on any map of the world. The Captain's party was the first to discover this uninhabited island. This island is under the dominion of no country, and by the rule of international law, "A newly discovered island on Earth is under the jurisdiction of the country of the discoverer." Naturally, this island should become a new territory of the Empire of Japan. Therefore, two years ago when the Captain landed with his party on this shore, his first order was to name this island *Asahi Island* and to declare it to forever be a territory of the Empire of Japan.

Since then, the shimmering Rising Sun flag has flown over the cape head on the coast. However, the entire objective of the Captain and his crew in landing on this island was to construct the secret Undersea Warship. And in the course of time, they will leave this island when the ship is complete. Of course, even after departing, there is no doubt that this place will forever be a territory of the Empire of Japan. Assessing the world's situation, a point of overwhelming anxiety is the competition in America and European countries over the borders of their lands and the competition over territories. Even though this island is uninhabited, when the sovereignty of a nation seems to be less than absolute, the rule of international law says nothing. Feigning ignorance, a new arrival will knock down the flag planted by a previous occupier and fly the flag of his own nation, and be ready for a rebuke in the form of a major conflict, during which, there is no benefit.

The fact is that, with unimaginable guile, Captain Sakuragi discovered this island, fair and square, and named it Asahi Island. Even if several Rising Sun flags were flown on the coast in order to show that this is a territory of the Empire of Japan, he was bothered by what may happen once he left. Of course, once we abandon this island, another country may not trespass in the next three to five years. But all peace of mind was eliminated with the sinking of the *Crescent Moon*. There is the precedent of Hideo and me drifting by chance to this island. After Captain Sakuragi and his crew succeed and leave this island, they will be replaced in time by the citizens of another nation because landing on this island is no longer unheard of. It would be awful if Americans and Europeans, who never tire of being acquisitive, land on this island some time in the future. Several hundred Rising Sun flags wouldn't bother them. They would shred the flags and replace them with the flags of the lion or the eagle, and occupy this island as if they owned it.

From our beginning, we have never shrunk from discord nor conflict. The truth is on our side, but after the only evidence, the Rising Sun flags, is removed on a desert island a great distance over surging waves, even if we had a million reasons, we have no proof, and obtaining the world's approval would probably be next to impossible.

This desert island may seem unimportant now, but thirty or fifty years from now when Japan is a dominant world power, we may understand how to readily make peace militarily with western Europe. But for now, the occupation of Asahi Island will continue and never pass to another country. Even after Captain Sakuragi and his crew leave, if the undeniable proof is rebuffed and another country attempts to encroach on this island, the plan described below must be carried out to establish this island as a territory of the Empire of Japan.

Captain Sakuragi took a breath and began, "Therefore, an ingenious plan has been devised." He chuckled, turned his head and said, "In fact, the developer of this plan was Seaman Takemura."

"Seaman, tell him the entire story."

The good-natured sailor began in his usual tone, "Well, I'm not so good at talking, so if you don't understand anything, just ask me until you do.

"Okay, here's my plan. As you know, Asahi Island is a dangerous place except near this house. If you trek ten or so miles deep into the mountains, long-nosed goblins or some other devilment may be lurking. No, no, there's nothing like that out there, nothing but some unknown number of poisonous snakes, gorillas, lions, and tigers. Even a reckless guy like me is too scared to go there and wouldn't make anyone else go either.

"So I was thinking that we can create a sturdy monument tower, carry it deep into the mountains, and erect it there. The name Asahi Island, our claim to this island as a territory of the Empire of Japan, and the date the island was discovered by Captain Sakuragi would be chiseled into the side of the monument tower. After we left the island, the arrival of foreigners wouldn't be a problem. Pulling down the Hinomaru flags on the shore and erecting the flags of the lion or the eagle would be pointless. The danger would keep people away from the site deep in the mountains where the monument tower would stand. If they can't go there, they won't know about this evidence.

"If they tried to go, they'd be devoured by savage

animals or poisonous snakes, naturally, there would be no dead bodies. So, if foreigners land on this island after we leave, any claim to being the first to discover it would be nonsense. We have the evidence. If they dispute us, we would offer to prove it and take them deep into the mountains to see the monument tower. What would they think when they read these words? 'On Meiji Year XX Month XX Day XX, Captain Sakuragi of the Imperial Japanese Navy discovered this island. This island is a territory of the Empire of Japan. All who follow shall take your flags and leave forthwith,' or something like that. That oughta scare them so much they'll faint. They'll be bowled over. That place will be like a slap upside the head."

"Aaah ha ha ha!" I howled. A truly ingenious plan. It sounded like a plan cooked up by the rugged Seaman Takemura. However, I pressed him with a few questions.

"How can we build this monument tower deep in those treacherous mountains? Do we intend to go to a place so dangerous the foreigners won't go?"

Seaman Takemura was not rattled. "For that, we have an incredible invention."

17

THE IRON ADVENTURE CAR

"**or that, we have** an incredible invention," said Seaman Takemura, unfazed. Triumphantly, he continued, "I haven't said anything reckless. The Captain feels this scheme is very clever."

"The Iron Adventure Car – We will build an automatic iron-cage car, load the monument onto it, and take it deep into the mountains."

"An...an iron-cage car?" I slapped my forehead.

After obtaining permission from the Captain, Seaman Takemura went to the adjacent room and returned with a draft drawing and spread it out on the table.

"This is it. The plan for the Automatic Iron Adventure Car. The iron-cage car looks like a wooden cow. It's 22 feet long, 13 feet wide, 12 feet high at the head of the cow, and $10\frac{1}{2}$ feet at the back end. Like it's name says, the four sides form an impenetrable iron cage. The floor is a resilient Krogh steel plate. Half of the top is covered by an iron plate and the rest by iron grating. The iron car is equipped with twelve wheels, between them are six gears. An intricate scheme applying various principles from physics produce the power for driving these wheels. Thirty-seven types of large, medium, and small gears engage with each other in a robust, elaborate machine, resembling a Nolden engine, that is installed in the front engine compartment.

"Various complex mechanisms resembling pistons, cranks, and a pelorus form a prototype steam engine. A man is seated in the chassis, clutches a handle with his right hand, and as he turns the steering wheel and slowly presses a peddle with his foot, a bell provided on his side immediately rings, the lower spindle begins to quietly rotate to send power to the first large gear, which transfers power to the second gear. Simultaneously, the pistons move up and down until the motions of the cranks become a blur. By the time the drive power reaches the thirty-seventh gear, the rotational speed and the power are intense. This extraordinary power rivaling that of a 440-horsepower steam engine passes through the pistons to drive the twelve exterior wheels and begins the advance of the rugged iron-cage car.

"This heavy vehicle is not very fast. It can travel an average of five miles per hour on a plain, but can barely manage one mile per hour on a steep path. "However, this Iron Adventure Car not only travels through water and up steep trails, it features six sturdy studded wheels in addition to the normal wheels, a spiral hoist mounted in front of the cab, and a transmission installed in the back for climbing steep mountains to draw power from the large trees and huge rocks along a mountain trail. The pointed screw tip bolts into a huge tree in front, then a hoist operates in the cab to naturally contract the screw to slowly lift the iron car. In contrast to the spiral hoist, the transmission abuts a rock behind the iron car to push the car forward by extending an elastic lever.

"To travel deep into the forest in the iron car, another

even more clever machine is provided. It consists of four huge rotating circular saws having twenty-one circular patterns that jut out above and below the head of the wooden cow of the iron car. This machine has eight sharp automatic rotating logging axes, which resemble the shape of the horrifying guillotine, said to have lopped off the heads of 13,000 people in the days of the French Revolution. Any huge tree blocking our progress would be felled from its trunk. Small trees, along with branches would be cut down. Therefore, we aren't the least bit worried about steep mountains or thick forests, because neither will stop our advance.

"It's a bit unusual, but the entrance and exit port of the iron-cage car is installed on the roof of the cab. We'll use an iron ladder to climb in and out. We want the port to be as impenetrable as the four sides of the iron cage. No matter how powerful the enemy is, we'll always be safe in the cab.

"The crew will have five men. In addition to the engine compartment, there are two compartments inside the car. One is neatly covered by a thick glass plate to keep out the elements. The floor will be covered by a rug or a blanket. This compartment is for the crew. The other is shaped like a travel trunk and will store ammunition, water, canned food, dried meat, and other supplies needed for the trip."

"It would be great if we could build this," said Seaman Takemura, looking at me while wiggling his nose.

"Wow! Fantastic! This invention is amazing!" I said not realizing I had been inching closer. The Seaman became more animated and said, "I'd like to try to build this automatic iron-cage car. No matter how dangerous a place is, we could go there. If a pack of gorillas or lions attacked, the menacing looks from the savage beasts would be met by bullets from the iron-cage car. We'll jump in this iron car and haul the monument tower engraved with the name Asahi Island about thirty miles deep into the mountains," then with confidence, he asked himself, "But is there a clever plan to put up the monument tower while surrounded by savage beasts and venomous snakes?...What? Takemura Shinpachiro is too dopey to come up with a plan like this?" He widened his eyes and looked around, then in a lowered voice said, "I'm not a braggart, but how could this kind of car be built? Well, I planned everything up to here, but all the vital mechanical inventions were devised by the Captain." He smiled wryly.

First, Captain Sakuragi then everyone else found this amusing and burst into laughter. An unperturbed Seaman Takemura looked at me and said, "You offered to work as a coal stoker or a cook, but you can't do such stupid work. A better job would be to start building this iron-cage car. The Captain had been planning this for a long time, and has already made draft plans. Unfortunately, he is busy with the Undersea Warship and can't divide his energy.

"Although he talked about starting the construction after the ship is finished, we have to return to Japan as soon as the Undersea Warship is done. So will you try? If you supervise this job and work as hard as you can, two or three of us will take turns working with you on our off hours. Around the time the Undersea Warship is finished, the iron-cage car will also be done. We can immediately get in and go deep into the mountains to erect the monument tower."

"Great!" I said, pumping my fist.

Captain Sakuragi smiled and asked me, "Are you willing to take on this responsibility?"

"I'll do it," I declared.

The Automatic Iron Adventure Car! Wow! Building the unprecedented iron car may not be easy. I'm just one man. For the next two years and nine months while the Captain and his crew engineer the astonishing Undersea Warship, I'll put my heart and soul into this task, although I'll meet obstacles, I will strive to do better than my best.

Captain Sakuragi was elated and said, "If you're determined to do this, we can find a place for you in the Secret Shipyard. I will provide you with sufficient materials and assign four sailors to help you everyday on alternating morning and afternoon shifts. And I'll advise you to the best of my ability."

"In that case, I'll work as if my life depended on it," I said, slapping my arm.

"Interesting," said Seaman Takemura stroking his beard.

Hideo, who had been politely standing next to Captain Sakuragi and intently listening to our conversation, seemed to understand the logic of our talk in his young heart. He turned his adorable face to me and said, "Hey, Uncle...if you're gonna build the iron car, I think...I think I can help."

"This has gotten very interesting," said Seaman Takemura as he picked up the boy.

Smiling, the Captain spoke, "More than an ironworker, Hideo must prepare to become a respected naval officer." He ruffled the boy's thick hair, who was now propped on the Seaman's knee, and looked at me and said, "I, Sakuragi Shigeo, will accept responsibility for Hideo's education and do my best to fulfill the wishes of his parents Hamajima Takebumi and Harue."

On hearing those words, my thoughts returned to my dear friend in Naples and his wife. My eyes welled with tears of gratitude for Hideo's fortunate fate of coming to an unexpected man in an unexpected place and fulfilling his father's wish for him to be entrusted to true men of the

Navy. For a time, the room was silent. Hushed strains of our national anthem *Kimigayo* were carried in by the breeze blowing in from the shore.

I looked out the window at the early evening on this thirteenth night of the lunar calendar to the moonlit blue water and white sands. Groups of sailors under the Captain's command were enjoying themselves after a day of hard work. Another group was reciting a Chinese poem. Yet another was performing a sword dance. One group of seven or eight sailors had formed an intimate circle on a section of the beach jutting out into the waves and were singing the stirring verse in *Kimigayo* that extolled prosperity forever.

"Magnificent!" I cheered.

Captain Sakuragi slowly rose and said, "Let's go join them and together shout *'Banzai!'* for the Empire.

BEGINNING THE NEXT DAY, from the dusky daybreak until the pitch black night fell on the starlit sea, I worked on the Automatic Iron Adventure Car. In the Secret Shipyard in the cave, the light of the fires blazing in the iron smelting furnace and the metallurgy furnace for the Undersea Warship or my work resembled the crimson tongues of evil spirits. The pounding hammers echoed through the lonely cave. The sea gods of Asahi Island must have been stupefied.

18

BASEBALL GAMES

One...two...three years passed. The Undersea Warship, which will shock the world, was 99.9% done, just as Captain Sakuragi had planned. Progress on our car kept pace, too. February 11, the auspicious day of Empire Day, neared. Five years had passed since the Captain and his crew landed on Asahi Island, and three years since Hideo and I landed. The automatic iron car under my charge was also finished. We will be delighted to drive the car before the test run ceremony to celebrate the warship's completion.

On reflection, those three years quickly passed. While on this desert island in the Indian Ocean several thousand miles from home, I often reminisced about the skies of home and recalled old friends, the beautiful sight of Shinagawa Bay in the morning, the bustling town of Ueno Asakusa, the new train stop at Shinbashi, sumo matches at Ekoin Temple, festival days in Kagurazaka, French stories published in the *Yorozu Choho* newspaper, the political speeches given at the Kinkikwan, the plays and *Naniwabushi* stories in song, and often eating at Yabu Soba and Baigetsu during my college years.

Even if I had wings and wanted to fly to the Japan I missed so much, these past three years were easy to bear for me. You, my friends, probably can't imagine this, but many interesting things have happened during that time. I went lion hunting dozens of times, and Seaman Takemura often had great success.

One time, we found the nest of a Steller's sea eagle in the grove right behind the house. You may not like this, but we took the eggs. Every morning, the Captain and his crew left for work. When they returned every evening at dusk along the still coast after toiling all day in the shipyard at the bottom of the sea, Hideo and Lightning would go to meet them. On hot days, they would bathe in the stream flowing behind the house. On cool days, they would enter the slightly extravagant bath prepared for them by Hideo and the sailors who remained at the house.

Days are long in the tropics, so about an hour after finishing supper, the Captain followed by the others would go out to the shore and indulge in outdoor exercise. There were areas for lawn tennis, cricket, a shooting range, and a sumo ring. Before leaving Japan, Captain Sakuragi made preparations for amusements to relieve the boredom of life on a desert island. The tennis court and the shooting range were well built. However, the most popular activities on the island were boat races and baseball games.

Boat racing is not a surprise given their profession, but the needed boats were destroyed by a typhoon. Only one gig and two cutters survived, and the oars were gone. So the fun boat races are no more. I watched them a few times, but they made do and there was always some pointless quarrel, and things didn't go as smoothly as boat races on the Sumida River.

Baseball doesn't have those kinds of problems, so it was always popular. The grounds were a rare flat field less than one tenth of a mile from the house. Shouts of "Out!" "Strike!" echoed from the field in the evening air. The umpire who was the only one dressed in black stood out. Captain Sakuragi was thirty-tree years old and a naval captain, but preferred games that mystified most Japanese, moreover, he was a skilled player. Long ago, he was a champion pitcher. He couldn't hide his face among his famous teammates, he looked the same.

I probably should tell you about the players on Asahi Island other than Seaman Takemura and me. That said, I hadn't touched a ball since I began globetrotting and my skills dwindled. However, if I played shortstop, we wouldn't lose to his mentors in the amateur club in Yokohama back home. Seaman Takemura's skills are phenomenal. Where does he practice? He throws nine terrifying, unhittable pitches with his iron-like arm. If the Seaman pitches, there are no rivals, and he couldn't keep from breaking bats. He usually bats left, and when the skilled pitcher throws a straight ball with all his strength, the ball would let out a groan as it flew off. If this ball hit you in the head, I think that would be your last glimpse of this world. You would feel awful and become helpless.

The Captain and his crew came to this island long before I arrived. While they've been here, the American battleship USS *Olympia* went to Yokohama. Six months before I drifted onto this island, I was in London, England and heard that the red-hot unhittable pitches of the celebrated Church defeated players from the First Higher School who were said to rule the baseball world in Japan. That was three or four years ago and truly regrettable.

High-ranking officers in the military probably wanted

to exact revenge. I secretly hope they still do. Some day after we leave this desert island and return to Japan, if Seaman Takemura visits each port in the world on a battleship or on the Captain's ship *Lightning* and arrives at the shores of North America, and if the USS *Olympia* dropped anchor anywhere, perhaps at the South Street Park in Vancouver or a beautiful open field at Golden Gate in San Francisco, with Seaman Takemura as our pitcher, the first-rate team of the famous Church would decide to compete in a spectacular match. Our rival, an American warship, and us, an Imperial Navy warship, would enjoy a sporting challenge on land without mines and gunfire.

Hideo is fantastic! He's also one of the players. At any time, he is the first to run out to the field. He's agile and unstoppable. He also possesses a phenomenal memory and instantly recalls any rule. Seaman Takemura said that he has a promising future as a player, but not only in baseball. Over the last three years, he has been educated by the solemn and merciful hand of Captain Sakuragi. He's now a twelve year-old youth who seems like a grown man. He has a dignified air and is self-possessed. He has become a brave youth, a replica of Captain Sakuragi.

In addition to boats and baseball, in his free time, Hideo throws rocks, climbs trees, and runs around the fields and mountains with Lightning. As a result, his build is amazing. And his face is pretty like a doll, but now he's a little tan. His mouth is firmly set, his eyes are bright. It's hard to describe his valiant appearance. If the opportunity comes, when he again sees his father Hamajima Takebumi, the father will be dumbstruck. And if the angelic Harue is safe and sees his brave figure, she will be pleasantly surprised.

Needless to say, Captain Sakuragi, the leader of this

island, is healthy and, these days, spends all day and all night at the Secret Shipyard. Seaman Takemura is funny and joking as always. The other thirty-six sailors are all in good health and work hard as they await the momentous day.

During these happy times, we finished the Automatic Iron-Cage Car and brought it out of the shop. The results of our test drive on the sheer cliff were good. The bell rang, and when the mysterious machinery switched on, the twelve outer wheels clawed the rock and dashed through the mud. It was as great as we expected and we couldn't stop cheering. Suddenly, someone called out and a group of sailors ran up and surrounded me.

"The iron car! *Banzai! Banzai!*" they shouted as they tossed me in the air. I was grateful for the cheers, but the tough men jostled me so hard from all sides I could barely breathe. Only Seaman Takemura wasn't convinced. With arms folded, he intently watched the operation of the iron-cage car, but immediately yelled, "Very good, it works well and isn't too slow," and quickly came running carrying the finished monument tower. The tower was 3 feet, 5 inches high and made from a marble slab. *Asahi Island — New territory of the Empire of Japan* was engraved on the smooth front surface. Clearly inscribed on the back were the date of discovery and the name of Captain Sakuragi, the discoverer.

Out of breath from hauling the tower, Seaman Takemura said, "Captain, if the iron car is finished, we shouldn't waste any time and immediately erect the monument tower while it's still light."

The Captain suppressed a laugh and said, "Of course, there is no need to delay. The Undersea Warship will have its test run ten days from now on Empire Day. Within a week after that, the plan is to complete all of the preparations and leave this island, so if we finish erecting the monument tower before then...," and to me he said, "Therefore, tomorrow at six in the morning, you will leave in the iron-cage car, and drive it seventy miles deep into the mountains. And at an average speed of 2.5 miles per hour, it should take two days to get there, one day to erect the tower, and two days to return. The iron car will return here on the fifth day, and we can shout *'Banzai!'*"

"Oh so, we have to wait until tomorrow?" Seaman Takemura said, slapping his palm, "Yeah, I don't agree with me either. Right now we need to prepare provisions and drinking water, and will set off in the morning." He was as funny as always.

It was decided that the iron car would leave the next morning at six to build the eternal tower monument at the top of a mountain. Since the launch ceremony for the Undersea Warship was approaching, Captain Sakuragi couldn't leave, not even for one day. Therefore, Hideo, Seaman Takemura, two other sailors, and I rode in the iron car. Thanks to pleading by Hideo, Lightning would accompany us on this adventure.

We loaded the monument tower onto the iron car and spent the day loading rifles, ammunition, drinking water, and food. The next morning, the selected five of us awoke before dawn and got into the iron car. Before long, when the iron car was about to set off, the more than thirty sailors, led by Captain Sakuragi, cheered us for more than a mile. At last, we said goodbye at the foot of a hill. We went east, and they went west. About halfway up the hill, we could no longer see Captain Sakuragi and his company waving handkerchiefs and hats nor the coconut palms and the flowers of the Chinese white olives. The iron car continued to advance at full speed over the fields and hills.

A description of the structure of the miraculous automatic iron car is not needed, it's fairly boring. But when we reached the forest, the actions of the rotating circular saws and the battle axes cleared a path. The six studded wheels joined by the actions of the hoist and the transmission, bit into the earth and smashed the rocks to climb the mountain. The forest became dense about ten miles short of the mountain, but Seaman Takemura remained in high spirits and somehow pushed us to cover more than fifty miles by sunset.

Although we were prepared for immediate attacks by savage animals and poisonous snakes when we entered the mountain, what we experienced was bizarre. An uneasy stillness surrounded us. The only sounds we heard were the creaking of the wheels and, from time to time, the sounds of a woodpecker drilling a tree trunk in the deserted forest. Nevertheless, the iron car kept advancing. When we reached the deep forest, Hideo tugged on my sleeve.

"A lion..."

"A lion? Where?" we asked together as we rose to look where he was pointing. On a patch of grass in a sunny spot about one hundred yards away, one large male lion was lying down, but was roused by the sounds of the iron car and roared.

"He's calling his friends!" whispered one sailor. A cry like distant thunder reverberated through the fields and hills. Soon savage creatures emerged from the shade of the rocks and formed groups of three to five. The lions, tigers, and gorillas were temporarily shocked by our mysterious iron-cage car and dared not approach.

An excited Hideo shouted, "Uncle, the lion may think we're goblins."

He was probably right. In a short time, large, snarling animals who had been hidden by the trees were glaring at us. The lion seemed to have summoned the rulers of all kinds of animals. Three or four of these courageous maned animals cried out and flew toward the iron car. The iron car was undaunted and launched bullets at the beasts. Even the kings of the beasts ended up rolling around in agony on the grass like dumplings. We burst into laughter. The tiger is a fairly stupid animal and couldn't resist jumping in a rage at the front of the car, and the fearsome rotating circular saws sliced off its limbs and ripped open its belly. He let out howls of pain as he was knocked down. The most cunning animal is the gorilla. He extended his hideous treelike arms and grabbed onto the cage of the iron car and, with all his might, tried to turn us over. The fierce Lightning gave him a savage bite.

"He's a bold one!" yelled a sailor.

In the instant I shouted, "Shoot him!," Hideo shot him three times, but the gorilla was untroubled. An angry Seaman Takemura yelled, "The savage is still alive?" grabbed a hand spear to pierce the beast's heart. Naturally, the gorilla was cut down, he groaned like thunder and crashed onto his back.

"Great! So, you are the King of the World. Now, these curious eyes can see no more." The two sailors were jubilant. Hideo gave a sideways glance at the gorilla's corpse and groused, "It's too bad my shots didn't kill him."

"No, it's not that. Mud and pine-tree gum has made this gorilla's fur as hard as iron, so no bullet from a rifle could easily pierce it," I said to cheer him up.

After the battle, the animals feared our power and did not readily approach, but they wouldn't leave either. They surrounded the iron-cage car and howled, but from a distance of thirty feet. Seaman Takemura opened his mouth wide and let out a great laugh.

"Hey! Hey! We probably look like delicious hunks of

meat to those beasts," he said as they crept closer to the iron cage.

"They can snack on this," he dared and thrust his iron fist out of the car. Just as the furious creatures leaped, he pulled his arm back in.

"Well, maybe not."

19

A BATTALION OF BEASTS

We witnessed another remarkable sight. A troop of about thirty white-headed langurs, intelligent monkeys that live deep in the mountains, appeared with the cold winds coming down the mountain, like a caravan trekking across the large Arabian Desert, riding on the backs of several a large elephants. Amazed by the sight of our iron car, they squealed and vanished into the thick forest.

By dusk, we had traveled close to fifty miles. We stopped the iron car to spend the night under the shade of a large tree and kept a watch fire burning all night. We intended to take turns sleeping in pairs, but the angry cries of the vicious animals kept everyone from a sound sleep. On the following morning while still dark, we left that place. Like the day before, several hundred of the beasts formed a battalion and pursued the iron car, but their fatigue allowed us to escape.

The bullets we continuously shot at them wounded and killed a few. And that day we traveled over fifty miles and were more than seventy miles away from the house on the shore. When we reached the peak of a high mountain, their ranks had thinned, but more than twenty male lions and three huge gorillas still lingered near the iron car.

The view at the mountaintop was astounding. We stopped the iron car on the summit at a location with a suitable geographical feature, a three-sided rock that formed a natural shrine. It was two forty-five in the afternoon when we began erecting the monument tower.

"Get ready!" called out Seaman Takemura. The two sailors came carrying a black box from inside the large trunk in the car. Several dozen bombs were in the box.

Dear Reader, You may be wondering, "Bombs! For what?" Much thought had been put into this operation. We couldn't get out of the car to do our work and erect this monument and achieve our objective while one or even two lions or gorillas were loitering nearby. So the plan was to toss out these bombs to kill or drive off the beasts and allow us to successfully complete our task. When ready, we each took a bomb in hand and stood. We ejected about thirteen pounds of chicken meat through the iron cage, and the famished beasts crowded together in a black mass to devour the meat. At the signal, 1...2...3, five bombs simultaneously cut through the air and dropped down. Immediately, black smoke and haze rose. Peering through breaks in the smoke, all three gorillas had been blown to pieces, and most of the lions were dead. At that moment, a sailor said, "Some of the lions are over there," when I looked to where he was pointing, a group of surviving lions was escaping through the haze into the forest.

"Now!" said Seaman Takemura and ran out carrying the monument tower, followed by the rest of us. Hideo kept watch. I dug up the ground. The sailors rolled over rocks. And Seaman Takemura barked random orders. We successfully erected the tower between struts. For ten minutes or maybe fifteen minutes, we worked as hard as anyone could. When finished, we took a few steps back to look at *Asahi Island – Territory of the Empire of Japan* clearly etched on the front of the gleaming marble tower. Relieved, we doffed our hats and cheered the Empire, "*Banzai! Banzai! Banzai!*"

Lightning, who we had left behind in the car, suddenly started to bark furiously. When I turned to look, the lions that had fled from the bombs had emerged from the forest and were charging directly at us. We all shouted in surprise and bolted in a panic for the iron-cage car. The danger was closing in fast. At the instant the top half of Seaman Take-mura made it into the car as he dove in last, a lion pounced, caught and shredded his pants leg, and savagely bit off a shoe, but he managed to tumble in with his life. I shot the lion as it leaped, and a sailor wildly speared him. Hideo sprung up and slammed the cage door shut.

"Well, I didn't expect that. They almost got us," said the shaken seaman. He looked where his shoe used to be and gratefully rubbed his uninjured leg.

Although we were given five days to go and return, we had already erected the tower and could return home. We were fortunate to have finished on the second day and could go home. With this kind of luck, if we dutifully retraced yesterday's route, by this time tomorrow, we would reach Captain Sakuragi's house on the coast, and our journey would safely end. However, men are inclined to seek adventure. But as some say, "Darkness follows light." I understand the logic, but this kind of trip is a once-in-a-lifetime opportunity. We still had three days until the fifth day when we promised to return. So I proposed taking a little detour into the mountains. It wouldn't make us late and would probably be fascinating.

I added, "How about it? We could return straightaway, but if we change our route just a little and returned through a new area, we would see many more curiosities than by returning the old way."

The inquisitive Seaman Takemura agreed without hesitation and with great enthusiasm said, "I was thinking that, too. The Captain doesn't think we'll return so soon. I expect that on the evening of the fifth day, the sailors will prepare a feast and be waiting for our return. And it wouldn't be any fun if we returned too soon, so we shouldn't be in a hurry to get back."

The two sailors and Hideo all agreed. We immediately began to discuss which way to go. We looked around in each direction. Several miles west of us stood a tall mountain, it appeared to be part of a chain of volcanic mountains. The top half of the mountain was sliced by red-hot stones, but at its foot was an endless forest. A large, swift-moving river cut through the center of the forest. We thought we would have many unusual experiences if we went that way. The sailors were given the order, and the iron car advanced in that direction. Along the way, wild animals appeared and disappeared from time to time.

It was close to six in the evening, and the sun was sinking behind the western mountains. Setting off into the forest at that time was rash, but we were ready to have fun and believed no enemies lurked there. When night fell, we had traveled two to three miles and were close to the forest.

The sickle-shaped new moon brilliantly lit the world, but not bright enough to guide our path. Also, every direction in this area was steep and covered with sharp rock edges and coiled tree roots. The iron car crawled forward, but the sailor driving the car seemed fatigued. It occurred to me that there are limits to a man's energy. As we plunged into the forest, I worried that we may have been a little too rash. When I suggested to Seaman Takemura that we spend the night here, he wouldn't listen.

"Don't go soft now. We're prepared to spend the night deep in the forest," he happily said and got up to relieve the driver.

Through its intense power, the iron car again moved forward by clawing the tree roots and biting into the rocks. He's a good man, I thought, a truly inspiring man, but his impulsiveness worries me, and we'll be fine as long as no emergencies arise. Suddenly, he cried out, "Dammit!"

Hideo, the sailors, Lightning, and I were flung forward. Seaman Takemura jumped down backward from the driver's cab, "Dammit! Crap!" he shouted as he hopped up. This was bad. The iron car had fallen into a large cone-shaped hole.

The sailors slowly got up and examined the hole in the faint light of the new moon and shouted, "We're in a quicksand sinkhole!"

Dear Reader, you may be familiar with adventure travel diaries that often describe places in the interior of Africa and islands in the Indian Ocean, and few places in the world are as terrifying as a quicksand sinkhole. It has another name, a death sinkhole. Once you've fallen into one, escape is impossible.

From the outside, the hole did not look very big. It had a diameter of thirty yards and a depth slightly less than its length. If we were on the roof of the car, we could have jumped out. However, the sides of the cone-shaped hole consisted of a fine sand. Not only is this sand fine, it possessed a strange kind of viscosity. Anyone who fell in would slide down as he tried to lift himself out and settle deeper into the sand. He wouldn't be able to freely move his arms and legs, and would eventually die an unnatural death. Now I understand why Captain Sakuragi repeatedly warned, "Watch out for quicksand sinkholes," when we left the house, but in the end, we fell into a terrifying death sinkhole.

"Damn, this is bad," said Seaman Takemura, cursing his mistake.

Although the iron car worked on steep mountains and thick forests, the only place it didn't work was in a quicksand sinkhole. Hoping against hope, we tried to turn the wheels any amount by using the car's phenomenal power, but it was no use. The useless studded wheels choked by sand barely inched forward and dragged the car up just three inches. As that happened, the other wheels were gradually buried in the sand and soon wouldn't budge.

"We're doomed!" we grieved.

If we had been in an ordinary place, we would have had a plan to escape by dumping the iron car and letting it fall into the jaws of death. However, we were deep inside many mountains and many peaks, and surrounded by the nests and haunts of wild animals and poisonous snakes for dozens of miles on all sides. By then, several dozen lions and gorillas had already surrounded the hole and were snarling, baring their fangs, and sharpening their claws. Even if we managed to get out by even an inch, a cruel death would be swift.

Although we were inside the car, the gorillas, known to quickly exploit man's weaknesses, leaped from the edge onto the roof of the iron car and, in a frenzy, reached into the iron cage to grab us. We shot at them and speared them, all while avoiding harm. But, how long could we last?

As the night wore on, the animals became more savage. At that time, we only kept the fire burning, and the watch fire we prepared steadily burned. From time to time, we would throw a leftover bomb. Unfortunately, the night would end eventually. The morning sun slowly rose over the peaks of the stark mountains in the east and illuminated our faces, but our expressions were blank. Hideo and the two sailors were silent. Laying beside me, Lightning seemed exhausted from barking all night. Only Seaman Takemura spoke. He could not bear that his mistake resulted in our plight. In desperation, he said, "I was so stupid. My mistake will kill you and Hideo, and I have no excuse for the Captain. This may or may not be an apology, but I'm going to take the risk and give my all to drive away these creatures."

He was about to jump out of the car when I commanded, "Stop! Don't be stupid.

"Seaman Takemura, even if you have the courage of a demon, how will you fight so many vicious animals?" I asked as I grabbed his shoulders and pulled him back. Suddenly, Lightning let out a piercing growl and stood up.

"I have a little plan," I said to everyone.

"A plan?" they all looked up.

"What I mean is, we must notify the Captain about this emergency to get his help."

"The Captain help us?" they looked puzzled.

I understood their qualms. The Captain's house was over seventy miles away. How could anything but a bird pass through these mountains to report the unexpected disaster that befell his men?

I proclaimed, "Lightning will be our messenger."

20

OUR MESSENGER LIGHTNING

An **anecdote from** the Austro-Prussian War of 1866 tells of an Austrian reconnaissance unit under siege by the enemy and forced to deliver a message to headquarters by concealing the secret dispatch in a military dog's collar. It is not uncommon to use dogs as messengers these days, but our situation is different. The two sailors were apprehensive, and Seaman Takemura's arms were folded as they sized up Lightning.

His head down, a distressed Hideo added, "So Lightning will leave us, and cross those scary mountains all by himself as the messenger to Captain Sakuragi. I'm worried. Is Lightning strong enough to get passed those wild animals in the mountains unharmed and get back to the house?"

His fears were reasonable. I understood the slim chances of a messenger in this kind of situation. Moreover, for over three years, we have gotten to know Lightning, and we love him so much we barely think of him as an animal and wouldn't want to see him experience even a little pain, but this was an emergency.

Extraordinary decisions must be made in an emergency. Any hesitation makes success hard to anticipate at the beginning, because none of us has complete knowledge, which disappears like dew on blades of grass in the mountains. But all possible measures must be tried. Tearfully, we decided that Captain Sakuragi, who was seventy miles away, had to be told of this sudden disaster, and Lightning would be our messenger through the perilous mountains. I quickly grabbed a pen and began to write. Here is the letter.

Dear Captain Sakuragi,

If there had not been a disaster, we would again be in your presence at the time this letter reaches you. We are sending this messenger because fate has not been kind.

We successfully erected the monument tower you had entrusted to us, but on the way back, we invited unexpected disaster. We fell into a terrifying quicksand sinkhole in the mountains about seventy miles east of your position on the coast. As implied by its other name, the death sinkhole, we soon became unable to move an inch. In addition, more ferocious attacks by wild animals have put the iron-cage car in grave danger. Only death awaits us now. With any luck, if Lightning hasn't been killed and this note about our predicament has reached you, we hope, Captain, you will devise a strategy to save us from this misfortune.

Hideo quietly said, "If this letter gets to my Uncle who is waiting for us to return today or tomorrow, he'll probably be pretty surprised."

Seaman Takemura nodded and said, "But I'm worried

that our courageous Captain may put himself in danger in his attempt to rescue us."

"We can't let that happen," I said and promptly added a few more lines.

> But given our situation, we have long prepared ourselves for the possibility that a narrow escape from death may be out of reach. The life of the man responsible for the success of the Undersea Warship is worth more than ten times our lives, and you should be reluctant to interrupt your mission that will benefit the Empire of Japan. We are concerned that you will brave great jeopardy to rescue us. If it is important for Japanese people to think of their country before themselves in any situation, the only just action if a rescue plan is not feasible would be to abandon us. We will be at ease with our fate, and our bones will be buried in this mountain.
>
> If we are unlucky and disappear with the mist in these mountains, on the day you will gaze from the splendid deck of the Undersea Warship at the ridges of the cotton roses, in place of the five of us, only one voice will cheer the Empire of Japan, but we will add our voices from the other world.

I finished the letter, folded it several times, and secured it to Lightning's collar. The dog looked up at me as I stroked his black fur, and as if I were speaking to a person, I said, "Lightning, because you are a superior dog, you probably understand our situation. Please don't give up. Please take this to the Captain."

As if he understood, Lightning gave his tail a dignified wag.

Hideo silently welled up and said, "Hey fellow, I'm sorry I can't go with you, but that's our fate. If we're lucky, you'll safely make it back to the Captain's house and save our lives, then we'll play on the beach again. If we're not so lucky and you die and don't get back, I'm gonna follow you to the next world and see you there."

The boy seemed to have prepared himself for that moment. Of course, the brave Seaman Takemura choked up and lamented, "I'm...I'm so sorry everyone. This is all my fault. Your misery was caused by my mistake."

But just as quickly he brightened.

"Well, enough of that, I can't sound like a woman," he cheered himself up and tapped the dog's collar.

"Lightning, don't give up," he said, looking into the dog's eyes.

Following my instructions, the two sailors picked up Lightning and placed him on the iron steps to allow him to leap forward from the top of the iron-cage car and out of the quicksand sinkhole. The mood of the wild animals outside the car changed as they watched us. When the sailors saw an opening and flung open the door, Lightning vaulted out and flew to the far edge. In a flash, several waiting lions sprang....5 seconds...10 seconds, a howl pierced the air. I thought Lightning had been brought down, but he was no ordinary dog. When he leaped out, I saw him clamp his mouth onto the throat of one lion and swing it around once. I managed to see him dart off pursued by a pack of lions that congealed into a black mass and disappear into the forest as I watched. As I expected, Lightning just may accomplish this critical mission. I became uncertain after thinking about it, but a sliver of hope remained. We intended to wait for Captain Sakuragi to somehow save our lives.

Three days passed with no news from the Captain, but we never expected it to be that easy. We endured days four, five, six, and seven in the mountains with no sign of rescue.

The strength of the iron car and plenty of ammunition kept us from being harmed by the savage animals, but another problem was building.

Our food and water had dwindled. As of yesterday, not even a steamed rice cake remained in the food box. The water barrel was dry and overturned in a corner of the iron car. All of us had reached the point of giving up all hope. Today, we had nothing to eat or drink. The night was sleepless, and we welcomed morning, but there was still no news. Gazing at the sky, the clouds were low. But we could hear the bloodcurdling cries of animals coming from just beyond the mountains. Our fate would soon be decided.

21

RESCUE FROM THE SKY

As I pondered our situation, today is the day before Empire Day, exactly nine days since we left the house on the coastline. Tomorrow was set as the day for the test run the Undersea Warship. If this mishap hadn't happened, we would be back at the Captain's house and looking forward to a pleasant day on the scenic shore. If we had obediently returned after erecting the monument, we would not be punished by regret now.

"Oh, there hasn't been any news yet. Lightning was probably killed on the way back," Hideo lamented and looked at Seaman Takemura.

"No, no, Lightning is an exceptional dog and probably has already reached the shore unharmed. But our disaster is extraordinary, so even the Captain couldn't just conjure up a rescue plan and has to think really hard about what to do. So don't give up. As long as you're alive, you can wait," said Seaman Takemura, deliberately upbeat, and grabbed the nape of the boy's neck as the two sailors exchanged sad glances.

A challenge too daunting may be impossible even for

the strong and wise Captain Sakuragi. If I disregard the lack of any news so far, an uninjured Lightning may have delivered the message, nevertheless, Captain Sakuragi is unable to mount a rescue. I had already convinced myself of this, but said nothing.

All of a sudden, the gang of animals surrounding the car were spooked, and growled and roared toward the sky. For an instant, we heard a faint gunshot, but couldn't pin down the direction.

We all jumped up and looked around, but saw nothing. We looked at each other confused, suddenly, another shot. Bang!

Seaman Takemura looked up and hollered, "A balloon! A balloon!"

I looked up toward the east and the dazzling sun and could make out a large balloon being carried by the wind toward us at a tilt, grazing the peaks of the stark mountains.

"Hooray! The Captain's come to rescue us in an airship!" shouted an ecstatic Hideo.

I yelled, "Hurry! Hurry! They're trying to locate us. Quick! We have to signal them."

Seaman Takemura and the two sailors tossed out a few of the remaining bombs. The echoes tumbled through the mountains and valleys, and a black smoke rose up. The pack of animals panicked and ran off. The men in the balloon seemed to have located us. A man's upper body appeared in the basket and frantically waved a white hand-kerchief from side to side.

The balloon slowly approached, and when it was fifty feet directly above us, a voice we had missed hearing, that of Captain Sakuragi, shouted, "Is everyone alright?"

At the same time, a sailor familiar to us all agilely

tossed out an anchor cable and skillfully locked it onto an end of the iron-cage car.

"Got it," they said together.

We pushed aside the door of the iron car and clambered up the rope like monkeys. At that moment, the animals that fled were emerging here and there from the forest. Upon seeing us slip into the sky, they howled eerily. All five of us had reached the balloon and were safe. More than being happy to see the Captain again, Hideo asked, "Captain, where's Lightning?"

The Captain laughed and replied, "He's safe. He's alright."

The two sailors and I were too happy to speak. Seaman Takemura apologized more fervently than before for his blunder, never looking up.

I'll leave to your imagination the extent of our joy and what we talked about, but I must tell you about one thing, the large balloon.

Captain Sakuragi recounted what happened. On that evening exactly eight days ago, that is, the evening of the day we dispatched our canine messenger, he immediately knew we had met with disaster because Lightning had returned covered in wounds and stained with blood.

The house was thrown into tumult. After many discussions, they decided that the only viable plan to rescue us from this danger was by balloon. However, a balloon is not easy to make. Fortunately, they happened to have brought all of the necessary materials from Japan to this island on the *Bay of Waves* and set to work immediately. Nevertheless, the work was formidable. They seemed to have used up a good part of the critical chemicals, and all of the 300 *yotan* of white silk they had hauled from Japan to decorate the interiors of the rooms in the Undersea Warship. He told the story, laughed and added, "As punishment for your curiosity that only brought disaster, you will have to endure unfurnished cabins when the Undersea Warship is finished."

All of us simply looked down.

"Yes, we'll do anything...," I replied. We had disrupted the construction of the Undersea Warship.

When I faltered trying to ask if we had seriously hampered the work, the Captain calmly replied, "No, we are on schedule. Tomorrow is the test run ceremony and within the week, we'll be able to leave this island.

"Hideo, soon you will see Mount Fuji that you have longed to see for so long."

We exchanged jubilant glances.

A euphoric Seaman Takemura shouted, "Wow, that's great. While you were making the balloon, you finished the Undersea Warship on time. While we looked like fools, the Captain and the other sailors labored without sleep."

Laughing, the Captain said, "Seaman Takemura, because of your mistake, the sailors had to work for eight days without a wink of sleep."

The Seaman hung his head low, and I was ashamed, too. As he spoke, the balloon flew at the mercy of the winds over the frightening mountains, forests, and valleys, leaving behind the iron-cage car that had served its purpose. Around 3:40 p.m., we again saw the beautiful coastline we had missed. It seemed like a dream. The sailors who stayed at the shore appeared to have spotted us and were waving hats and handkerchiefs from the sheer cliff and from the Captain's house. They pointed to the shore where the balloon was descending and raced there like ants. Leading the way and kicking up a cloud of dust was, without a doubt, Lightning in full gallop.

We landed on the shore about 500 yards from the house. The excited sailors greeted us as we climbed out of the balloon. The first thing Hideo did was hug Lightning around the neck. The two sailors sprinted after their fellow sailors and ran about while shouting happily. The "celebration of their narrow escape from death" was a flurry of swinging fists, so the two sailors soon fled screaming, "Enough!" Of course, it was all in fun, but exasperating.

When the smiling Captain slowly stepped out, everyone surrounded us, and we set off for home. On the way back, Seaman Takemura was delighted and encouraged everyone from his spot in the center, waving his hands and talking nonstop, beginning with the tale of our adventure. Being an honest man, in a voice louder than most, he bragged about his exploits in driving off the gorillas as well as his fiasco of a plan.

Of course, we were elated when we arrived at the Captain's house, like seeing clear skies after the torrential downpour of a violent storm. Whether for the celebration of our narrow escape from death or for tomorrow's preparations, excitement ruled from that moment on.

22

DISASTER AT SEA

February 11, the long-awaited Empire Day had come. Last night, the activities didn't die down until midnight, but today no one overslept. I awoke at dawn and ran out to the beach where Captain Sakuragi, Hideo, Seaman Takemura, and the sailors were all smiles as they strolled along the shore. The bright morning sun rose faraway in the east above the vast sea and seemed particularly bright today. Back home around this time of year around sunrise, from the bustling Miyakooji Street to a humble cottage deep in the forests, the Hinomaru flies high above every door at every house to celebrate the prosperity of our nation.

Even on this far-off desert island in the Indian Ocean, we couldn't let this day pass without celebrating. On this day last year, this day the year before, and today, we took the day off and celebrated in our hearts. For us, this year, that day is not only a national holiday, it may also become a lifelong celebration. As the day on which the Undersea Warship was completed and surfaced for the first time in the ocean, our celebration would be memorable. We spent last evening decorating the shore of Asahi Island wherever we could reach.

Rising Sun flags encircled the Captain's house with no gaps. A magnificent greenery arch festooned the front. A tall flagpole had been erected on the end of the headland where the wave surges broke. The flags of all the world's nations were hastily attached to lines pulled in three directions from the top of the pole and fluttered in the wind. Our celebrated Rising Sun flag flew on top, as if looking down on the world's nations.

Along the beach, blankets, sailcloth, and various weapons had been beautifully arranged on the fine sand to depict Mount Fuji; the evening landscape of Futamigaura; and Kato Kiyomasa, the eradicator of tigers.

I wondered what a group of boisterous sailors was doing off in the distance at the foot of a small hill covered in luxuriant green palms and olives. The view was striking in all directions. A camp was being built for the evening's celebrations. Much activity centered around bringing out sailcloth, old masts, chairs, and tables.

At nine that morning, we heard a gunshot when the Undersea Warship was to leave The Secret Shipyard. Captain Sakuragi, who had returned to the house, was dressed in the brilliant gold-braided uniform of a navy captain. He gave orders to a group of sailors and entered The Secret Shipyard below the sheer cliff.

Hideo, another group of sailors, and I stood on the shore waiting to set off fireworks, wave flags, and cheer as we witnessed the test run. At half past nine, a second shot rang out, and our amazing Undersea Warship launched into the sea. The sight of all one hundred thirty feet of the flawless *Lightning* ship silently floating on the waves was inspiring. Standing on an unseen platform, Captain Sakuragi held his saber high, shouted a command, and the ship hurtled at full speed into the sea like a meteor. On the second command, we saw the deck smoothly close and mist spray into the air.

The ship abruptly dove below the waves, resurfaced, dove again, went left and right, and forward and backward. You would suspect the work of demons seeing this ship disappear and reappear in unexpected places. Far off in the bay, several whales blowing seawater resembling a small mountain began to swim toward the ship. The number of animals was not small. They reminded me of a squadron of a hostile nation. The funnel-shaped ram of *Lightning* began to move and lunge forward as quick as lightning. Soon the five to seven large whales, kings of the ocean, were mincemeat and stained the waves with their blood.

The ship darted along the bottom of the sea like a dragon, aimed two shots at a huge rock on the ocean surface, and, through the power of the innovative fish-shaped torpedoes, sent rock fragments flying into the shredded waves. Cheers erupted on the deck of *Lightning*. At the same time, all of us watching from the cliff shouted *Banzai!*, set off fireworks, and frantically waved our flags. Hideo was mesmerized. And the dog Lightning flew out to the shoreline and dashed around, like a streak of lightning.

This was probably our greatest success since coming to the island and concluded the test run of the Undersea Warship. Captain Sakuragi ordered the crew to dock the ship. Like a warrior taking a rest, *Lightning* came close to shore and dropped anchor.

From that moment on, we celebrated Empire Day and the great achievement of the day. The grand banquet commenced in the camp by the shore. No words, written or spoken, could describe the festivities. Some sailors performed farces, and others played military music.

Seaman Takemura recounted a verse of *Kawanakajima* while accompanying himself on the *Satsuma biwa* lute. Until that day, I never realized these men had these hidden talents, in particular, Captain Sakuragi's recitation of a Chinese poem in his resonant voice as Hideo performed a heroic sword dance was the jewel of the evening. Accomplished in nothing, I could only demur and provide thunderous applause and ovations.

The revelry ended a little after eleven that evening. To guard the deck of the Undersea Warship that had surfaced and was bobbing on the sea, the Captain posted a crew of sailors commanded by Seaman Takemura to the ship. The rest of the sailors, Hideo, and I had no reason to board the ship, so we returned home. This is probably true for everyone, but it's hard to go straight to sleep after a boisterous day. So back at the house that night, everyone gathered in one room and chatted about many things.

I looked out the window and saw *Lightning* serenely bobbing on the waves, bathed in starlight. Not only was the ship finished, in one week, in less than ten days, all the preparations would be complete and we could leave this island. We would leave at the colossal speed of 100 knots per hour, cross the Indian Ocean, pass through the China Sea, and ride on the waves of the dearly missed Sea of Japan and, for the first time in a long time, look at the ridges of the cotton roses.

The guileless sailors imagined what that scene would be like. The conversations never faded, but were filled with the men's assessments of the ship *Lightning*, the glory of Captain Sakuragi, and the various pleasures in each man's heart. If someone had told Hideo and I, who once thought we would die, that we would reappear in the world unharmed on the ship *Lightning* and return to Hamajima

Takebumi and, if she survived, Harue in Naples, we would have been astonished and delighted.

Thinking about this, you may realize that the gleam of happiness shining in our eyes may cause the hand of a demon jealous of human happiness to summon some calamity. Moreover, a crisis never fails to occur at the height of joy.

But even the grasses and the trees sleep. During a lull in the conversations between one and two o'clock, we could barely make out a sudden rumbling sound coming from somewhere. The sound resembled the echoes of claps of thunder. At that moment, Lightning began to bark wildly. We jumped to our feet. The echoes above the sea sounded like the celestial axis was rupturing. A gust of briny air with a spray of waves rushed into the room.

"Tsunami! Tsunami!" we all cried out.

Bewildered, we rushed outside. It looked like black ink was flowing on one side of the fiery sky lit by the Big Dipper. The vast surface of the ocean had swollen into a misty sky. We later found out that this tsunami had been caused by a landslide on the bottom of the sea near the Maldives in the Indian Ocean. Areas from the coast of Africa to Arabia were ravaged, and its surge reached as far as this desert island.

This was an emergency! Luckily, our house had been built on top of a cliff, so we escaped being sacrificed to that fearsome evil. However, our first concern was the safety of the Undersea Warship and the whereabouts of the Captain and the other sailors.

The dark sky blended into the ground. The ocean surface was a whirlpool of billowing waves. I could barely see an inch in front of me and anxiously lit a lantern and ran out. Hideo and the sailors were all holding torchlights and standing at the edge of the cliff, yelling as loud as they could while waving their lights all around. The waves drowned out our shouts, but we could discern a pinprick of light far offshore. It was definitely the night signal from the Undersea Warship! The signal meant that *Lightning* was safe! *Lightning* was safe!

23

TWELVE BARRELS

The tsunami had turned the landscape into a wasteland.

The next morning, the sea had almost returned to normal. As far as my eyes could see, the shore had been ruined by the stormy waves; the scene was desolate. Yesterday's ornate figure of Kiyomasa built on the sand, the landscape of Futamigaura, and the camp of coconut palms had all been swept away. The Secret Shipyard seemed to have been briefly flooded with seawater. The morning sun reflected oddly off the water droplets falling from the tangled seagrass dangling off the brow of the cliff high above the sea.

Lightning moved closer to shore. Captain Sakuragi came ashore with his crew, and we immediately ran over to them. We were ecstatic the Undersea Warship was undamaged. My face brimmed with joy as I grabbed the Captain's hand. We were all relieved that no one had been hurt by the disaster. As I looked at the Captain's face and asked, "What did you see on the ocean last night?" what I saw surprised me. The Captain's usual composed and collected look appeared anguished, unsure. Not only the Captain, the usually upbeat Seaman Takemura, and the other sailors who had been on Lightning were pale and looking down, like they were deep in thought. I was alarmed and immediately asked, "Did something happen? Was the Undersea Warship damaged during the tsunami?"

"No," replied the Captain, lifting his head slightly, he fixed his gaze on me, "Nothing is wrong with *Lightning*'s hull, but...but I believe that the tsunami has knocked all of us out of the heaven of hope down into the valley of despair."

"Wh...Why?"

The complexions of his crew changed for a moment. The Captain didn't respond right away, but turned his head to look at the cliff. The cheerless Captain asked, "Did you inspect the interior of The Secret Shipyard this morning?"

"No, not yet," I replied.

I thought that if the tsunami had occurred two or three days ago while the Undersea Warship was still in dry dock, an inspection would have been urgent, but not so much now. There was no need to rush to inspect it. But I surmised from the Captain's words and demeanor that the source of his anguish was that place, and quickly added, "I haven't looked yet, but as you see, seagrass has been propelled onto the edge of that high cliff. Therefore, the interior of the Secret Shipyard may have been heavily damaged by the infiltration of seawater. Is there a reason to be so worried?"

"Of course," said the Captain, placing his hand on his chest.

"Have you forgotten? The life of the Undersea Warship is still inside The Secret Shipyard."

"The life of the Undersea Warship?"

"The twelve barrels. As you know, all of the machinery in the Undersea Warship operate by the actions of twelve secret chemicals. The chemicals that give rise to these actions are sealed in the twelve barrels stored in a section of the shipyard. But during the tsunami, one may not have been safe. No, not one of them was safe."

"What!?" we were all stunned and realized how bad things were. The Captain let out a deep sigh.

"Perhaps I am wrong. In fact, a calamity from the heavens does not rival the abilities of men, but experiencing this disaster was lamentable. If all twelve barrels have been washed away, the miraculous and mysterious powers of the Undersea Warship are no more. This is exactly like an ordinary steamship running out of coal and coming to a stop on the ocean, and left to decay. Of course, a small amount of fuel loaded in *Lightning* for the test run remains. That remaining bit would last a little over 1,000 nautical miles.

"The nearest inhabited location that far from this island is in the sparsely populated Maldives. We could probably reach Kanran Island, but there is no suitable destination there. It would be awful to get stuck there and invite catastrophe. Kanran Island is desolate. It would be impossible for us to obtain chemicals there. Moreover, we would be unable to communicate with the other islands or the continent to obtain supplies.

"Also, notorious pirate ships are constantly on the prowl near Kanran Island. Therefore, frequent patrols are conducted by the warships of various European nations. Nothing would be more reckless than to enter that region and have the machinery on the Undersea Warship stop, and the ship surface there.

"If they knew we had completed the warship for the Empire of Japan, they would never stay silent, and a full-scale attack would be inevitable. If they made their move while the peerless *Lightning* had no power, we could do nothing. We wouldn't hesitate to openly sacrifice our lives there, but they would plunder the Undersea Warship. Our hard work over many months would become foam on the water. Our plan for our beloved Empire of Japan would become a sharpened sword handed to a foe.

"How could we do that? After we exhaust all of our resources, we will rot away forever on this desert island with the Undersea Warship. It would be reckless to leave this island. We can't leave. That is it.

"If The Secret Shipyard has been destroyed by seawater, as I believe it has, and even one of the twelve barrels was washed away, we won't be able to go even one foot away from this island. Our earnest, joyous hope of returning to Japan has been snatched away."

"Oh no!" we cried out. Everyone was stunned.

We knew that none of the barrels remained on the landscape devastated by the tsunami. But we thought there was an outside chance. We ran to The Secret Shipyard in the cave. Unfortunately, the Captain was right. The interior was wrecked. The waves had smashed through a rock wall. A torrent of water inundated the space, and in no time blasted through the iron door of the small storeroom housing the chemicals and pushed the twelve barrels to places unknown. Neither shadow nor shape remained.

The Captain was dispirited and only looked up to heaven. The color drained from all our faces. We had been dropped from heaven to the depths of hell. People are not made for this kind of despair.

There was nothing we could do, so we returned to the house. The atmosphere was dismal like after a destructive fire has been extinguished. The silent Captain Sakuragi was deep in thought. Seaman Takemura welled up with tears of regret and stared with venom at the choppy seas.

"Well, we can no longer go home to Japan," he said, gazing in vain at the eastern sky. I couldn't imagine what was in his heart. The other intrepid sailors had silently formed into scattered groups and only looked at each other. Two or three sailors trotted around looking for one or maybe two barrels. Of course, it was hopeless.

24

A BALLOON FLIGHT

I **brooded over our** situation and concluded that this may have been an inevitable calamity from heaven. As Captain Sakuragi said, aside from leaving this island at great risk, there is no other plan. The twelve chemicals that yield the actions of *Lightning* could not be manufactured on this desert island no matter how long we tried. Even without replenishments of our supplies, we may survive another ten or twenty years. Day and night, we would look on the unrivaled *Lightning*, but end up as the demons of this isolated island. These thoughts anguished me. I yearned for the skies of home. As silent tears formed, Captain Sakuragi who had been absorbed in thought suddenly looked up. He had a plan.

With a determined look, the Captain spoke, "Our present misfortune leaves us with two possible paths. One is to accept our fate and turn to dust on this island with *Lightning*. However, who would want that? There is only one other plan, an emergency measure. We have the large balloon we constructed to save you after the automatic iron car plunged into the quicksand sinkhole on that unlucky day.

"My plan is for two men to fly the balloon to Colombo in India or some other city on the continent and buy the twelve chemicals needed for *Lightning*. From there, they will secretly load the chemicals onto a ship and transport them to Kanran Island, which is 1,000 nautical miles away from here, exactly halfway between the continent and this island. Around the time the transport ship reaches Kanran Island, *Lightning* will set off from here and use up the remaining fuel to rendezvous with the transport ship. The chemicals will be transferred onto *Lightning*, then we will return to Japan.

"Of course, success or failure is difficult to predict. Unless the mission fails because the balloon ruptures during flight, or some other mishap occurs, *Lightning* will leave this island on the promised day and proceed to Kanran Island. We would be able to guess the balloon's fate if we wait for several days and no ship arrives, and we would be resigned to our fate. Our final mission will be to keep the secret of the Undersea Warship from the pirates and from the warships of powerful foreign nations. We will prepare to destroy the ship with explosives and cast it into the abyss.

"Although this is an extreme measure, at this time, we have no goal and no hope, and this will put an end to our dilemma. Rather than rotting in vain on this desert island while looking at the Undersea Warship floating before our eyes, this is clearly the path we have to take."

The unshakable Captain stopped and surveyed us.

No one intended to object to the Captain's words. The decision was made. Next, he had to decide who would take the balloon and carry out this mission. The brave sailors rushed forward to be chosen. However, the Captain could not make this decision lightly. This mission was too important. After the balloon lands in some city on the continent, the maneuvering required to purchase the secret chemicals, covertly load the chemicals onto a boat, and set sail for Kanran Island is not trivial. I understood the Captain's concerns and put myself forward.

When I said, "I may be unworthy for this critical mission, but I would like to volunteer," the Captain seemed pleased.

"The fact is I was waiting for you to speak. This task cannot succeed through courage alone. The balloon will land in a foreign country. I could only rely on you to handle the foreign language and other aspects of the mission," he said as he glanced around.

"Now, who will be your assistant?"

The reinvigorated Seaman Takemura stepped forward and said, "I will go."

The Captain fixed his eyes on the Seaman's face and said, "The success of this mission will be determined by whether our Undersea Warship can emerge in the world to protect the Empire of Japan. You must exercise extreme vigilance and caution."

The Seaman said nothing. His tears fell as he turned to look at the Captain.

Now that Seaman Takemura and I had been assigned this duty, Captain Sakuragi and the others, who would remain on this island, had to work out the details with us. Today is February 12. Because the wind direction is favorable, if we launch the balloon today and cross the skies of the Indian Ocean, we will probably land close to Colombo, the nearest city on the continent, on the sixteenth or seventeenth. Before we could go to Kanran Island, we would need five days to procure the secret chemicals and hire a ship. If we planned to reach the island between the twenty-fourth and the twenty-seventh or -eighth, the Captain and crew promised to board *Lightning* at midnight on the twenty-fourth and leave this island, and arrive at the lee of Kanran Island by dawn on the following day. Whichever side reached the island first would wait a week for the other. If the other side does not appear after the week has passed, we should already be prepared for our fate.

When we finished, at the Captain's order, we dragged the balloon onto the beach, filled it with hydrogen, loaded the basket with several days of provisions, and a large quantity of gold and silver for buying the chemicals and hiring a ship. Seaman Takemura and I prepared light travel kits and climbed into the basket.

We didn't know if this parting would be forever. Captain Sakuragi and Hideo just looked at us and vigorously shook our hands. The sailors I had come to know well over the past three years were reluctant to see us go and surrounded the balloon. No one said a word. Emotions ran deep, and tears flowed down a few cheeks. The Seaman and I cried in our hearts. Everyone's silence meant more than a thousand words.

Meanwhile, the tether ropes were untied, and the balloon began to rise. The Captain and the sailors all waved handkerchiefs. Seaman Takemura and I took off our hats and waved down at them. The winds blowing from south to north slowly carried us along at three thousand feet toward the continent. Our home, Asahi Island, became a pea on the endless horizon, then disappeared.

25

A WHITE PATROL SHIP

Three days had passed since we left Asahi Island. We crossed the skies of the Indian Ocean and were almost 5,000 miles north of Captain Sakuragi's house. In a far-off corner of the sky, we noticed the shadow of the continent that resembled clouds or smoke. Seaman Takemura and I exchanged glances and took deep breaths. Without a doubt, we were looking at the Indian continent.

Three or four hours from now, we would land near our target, the city of Colombo, and be able to complete the important task entrusted to us by the Captain. As we enjoyed this moment, catastrophe struck again. This was unbelievable. We had been traveling due north from the south up to then, as if favored by heaven. But the winds that had been steadily blowing the balloon toward the continent abruptly shifted into east-to-west winds.

When we left Asahi Island, Captain Sakuragi made atmospheric observations and advised us that there probably wouldn't be severe changes in the wind direction over the next three or four days. However, predicting the direction of the wind was as hard as predicting an act of heaven. The easterly winds had changed the direction of the balloon, and we were now being carried oblique to the continent toward the ocean. We blanched as our joy was replaced by fear and shock.

What will happen now? Has heaven cursed us? We chafed at our predicament and fought, but to no avail. As we watched the shadow of the continent vanish from view, the winds strengthened and transformed into a notorious typhoon. I became dizzy looking down at the world below. As far as I could see, the ocean surface filled with savage waves. The grim scene tricked my eyes into seeing tens of thousands of leaping white dragons, as the winds shrieked and the white clouds ripped apart.

A whirlwind does not move in one direction, but to the west, east, north, and south. The balloon bounced up and down in the sky like goose down and flew at a tilt over the many islands of the Maldives. The Laccadive Islands sped by like meteors. Where were we headed? We soared through the sky as if in a nightmare for four days and nights. On the morning of the fifth day, the winds had calmed, and the trembling of the balloon stilled. We felt reborn.

We inched up and cautiously peered from the basket, but had no idea where we were nor whether east or west winds were blowing. We had been blown out over a boundless sea. Where were we? We looked around, but could not find any clues.

Seaman Takemura thought we had been blown west across the African continent and were now looking down at the Atlantic Ocean, but I disagreed. A whirlwind would have blown a balloon around and around the same area, so we didn't have to worry about being carried far away. I believed we were over the Indian Ocean, perhaps, west of

Madagascar or above the Gulf of Aden, but not as far off as the coast of Europe.

However, I had no time to mull this over. We had bigger problems. The deadline set by Captain Sakuragi was drawing near. According to the plan, we had until the twenty-fifth to land near Colombo, buy the secret chemicals, load them onto a ship, and arrive at Kanran Island. We only had six days left. On the appointed day, the Captain with Hideo and the others would board the Undersea Warship and leave Asahi Island and secretly arrive at Kanran Island. Today or tomorrow, they'll be waiting for our support.

Will we be able to carry out our mission in our current situation? We drifted through the big sky of unending clouds and smoke. We couldn't tell whether we were heading east or west. When will we reach the continent? If we don't meet the goal of reaching Kanran Island and only helplessly watch as the deadlines of the twenty-fifth and the weeklong wait pass, the Captain will be prepared to drown and disappear with the incomparable Undersea Warship.

Our situation was urgent. Distressed about not knowing our position, I looked at Seaman Takemura. Just then, I saw what appeared to be a wisp of clouds on the distant horizon. I couldn't tell whether it was a bird or a ship. A lone white dot steadily neared. It was a white patrol ship. The flags flying on the gaff were still indistinct, and we couldn't identify the country of that vessel. She slashed through the waves toward us, belching black smoke. I immediately devised a plan. We had been assigned a critical mission, but could only drift not knowing when we would reach the continent. I did not want to feel the bitter regret of missing the rendezvous. Although we had no idea where the white patrol ship came from or where it was going or what nation it belonged to, we had to seek its help.

Naturally, we couldn't reveal the objective of our flight or the secret Undersea Warship of Captain Sakuragi to a foreign ship, but we did have the tactics of adapt and evade. If we were saved by this ship and taken anywhere on a nearby continent, the promised provisions could be gathered by the deadline, and we could arrive at Kanran Island where Captain Sakuragi would be waiting.

I spoke with the Seaman and he agreed. He immediately started waving around a white handkerchief to signal distress. The white patrol ship seemed to have detected our balloon. We saw a white and red flag on its deck being moved vertically. Seaman Takemura spotted something and screamed so loud, I thought his voice would break.

"Oh no! No! Not now!"

Frightened, I turned to look toward the patrol ship, but saw nothing to be worried about. But when I looked to the western skies, Danbrow birds, giant seabirds native to the Indian Ocean and armed with sharp beaks, long talons, and a large seven- to thirteen-foot wingspan, had formed a flock so large they blocked the sun. They had spied our balloon and were on the attack.

We were stunned. This type of seabird is not savage by nature, but if we fell from this height, who knows if we would escape unharmed. I lost my composure. With no time to think, I had to rout them, but accidentally fired the rifle once. Amazingly, the bullet caught one bird. But at the same time, another flock became hostile towards us. Three or four angry birds flew like an arrow toward the balloon. Soon, their beaks had torn it. By then, the patrol ship was a little over a nautical mile away and seemed to grasp our plight.

Seaman Takemura recognized the ship's flags on the gaff and yelled, "Hey! Hey! Those flags! That boat!"

He forgot our dilemma and started to leap around. I turned to look, but it was too late. The balloon had been ripped open by the Danbrow birds and was plummeting down, accompanied by the swishing sound of escaping hydrogen gas. Before we knew it, we crashed into the sea.

26

FACE TO FACE

We plunged into the sea with the balloon and, for a short time, fell several dozen feet toward the sea floor. Fortunately, the speed of our drop was slowed by the drag of the balloon in the waves, so we escaped death and in a short time were floating on the surface again. We swam for our lives and soon heard voices calling us from above the waves and the sounds of approaching oars. A small boat had come to our rescue. Our narrow escape would be aided by a boat from that white patrol ship.

As Seaman Takemura was pulled into the boat, he yelled, "Just as I thought! The flags on the gaff of that patrol ship are the naval flags of our Empire."

The instant he fell from the balloon, he recognized in a glimpse the familiar pattern of naval flags at the bow of this boat. I noticed the same thing after I got into the boat and jumped up in surprise.

"Ah! Soldiers of the Empire! Sailors of the Imperial Navy of Japan!" I cried out.

I turned and saw the white patrol ship floating like a small mountain on the sea not far from us. On the gaff and the stern, the naval flags of the Empire of Japan glimmered in the morning sun as they fluttered in the south winds.

The seaman gripping the oars on the port and starboard sides of the boat stared at us with surprise tinged with suspicion. A darkly tanned lieutenant with sea air blowing through his bristly beard commanded the helm at the stern, lengthened his imposing figure and simply asked, "So you're Japanese, too?" and stared at our faces. Further inquiries were not possible as the boat was jostled by the rough waves covering the ocean surface from the east to the west. As he spoke, a large swell crashed into the boat nearly capsizing it. The lieutenant turned the tiller starboard and called out, "Forward!" The bow of the boat turned and advanced like an arrow toward the patrol ship accompanied by the sounds of twelve oars cutting the waves.

Seaman Takemura and I felt like we were dreaming in a dream. I also forgot that I felt like a drowned rat with a stomach ache, having gulped down quite a quantity of seawater. I smiled to myself as I stared straight ahead at the white patrol ship, its gaff flying the familiar flags of the Imperial Navy. The ship was unable to cast anchor in this deep part of the sea and drifted left and right like a small trembling mountain. That magnificent vessel was an armored two-funnel cruiser with a displacement of just 2,700 tons.

While being tossed about by the waves, I could read the three characters for *Sunrise* (Hi-No-De; 日 の 出) on the stern radiating in the sunlight as they circled us.

"The warship *Sunrise!* The warship *Sunrise!*" I repeated to myself not knowing why, as we slowly approached the ship. A large crew stood in formation on the deck of the *Sunrise* from the bridge at the stern to the bow where the flags flew to receive our returning boat. Just before we reached the ship, the sea slowly lifted and lowered the huge 2,700-ton ship as if seawater from the deep was moving. And our small boat kicked up waves resembling leaves falling from trees in autumn. This prevented us from getting close to the port-side ladder. Sea mist flew around us, and the choppy seas smashed into us. Near the gangway above us close to the bulwark, another lieutenant was continuously barking orders at the sailors.

The lieutenant at our bow gripped the hilt of the tiller that had just broken off, danced in the air and fell into the abyss. The boat smashed several times into the waterline armor of the ship. I only exhaled again once a crane had hoisted the boat with its more than a dozen occupants back onto the deck of the *Sunrise*. On command, the ship kicked up a screw wave and began to advance. The discipline on deck was not disturbed by this spectacle.

"A balloon fell from the sky. A boat was lowered from this ship. The two men rescued are Japanese. One is an adventurous looking young gentleman. The other is a sailor in our Navy. That's strange."

This rumor had spread throughout the *Sunrise*, but no one forgot his duty wondering "Who? What men?" nor became the least bit undisciplined as they rushed to our rescue. The firemen maintained the engine room. The signal man stood in the lookout tower. First class, second class, and third class sailors handled the lowered boat under the commands of the lieutenant. A party of off-duty officers and sailors directed us to a special cabin. There we exchanged our wet clothes for new ones. One sensible officer kindly gave each of us a glass of brandy to calm us. I only marveled at the dignity of the military discipline I witnessed.

Lieutenant Whiskers who commanded the boat that

saved us looked at our faces restored to their usual colors and briskly stepped forward. As a smile rose on his face, he said, "I congratulate you two on your good luck."

As he turned to look from side to side, a navy captain descended the bridge at the stern and strode toward us. He was the captain of this ship, an impressive, dignified man with a ramrod posture. The Captain had been informed by Lieutenant Whiskers about the two Japanese who fell from the sky in a balloon, and appeared to know that one was an adventurous-looking young gentleman and the other a sailor in his Navy. He stood before us staring at our faces and didn't seem surprised. With a nod he directed us to sit down, twisted his mustache, and calmly turned to us. We respectfully bowed. I was struck by his face. The Captain's eyes and mouth reminded me of someone. Who was it? Unfortunately, no one came to mind.

When I calmly assessed our situation, our rescue from peril by our fellow Japanese men of the heroic Imperial Navy was not mere luck. The loyalty of Captain Sakuragi still being tested by heaven on Asahi Island should not be overlooked. We remembered and were unexpectedly moved to tears. As I nodded and glanced sideways at Seaman Takemura, three sailors standing at attention beside us heard some order given by the Captain and stared harder than before at Seaman Takemura. One sailor took a step forward and addressed Lieutenant Whiskers and the Captain, respectfully and with an air of significance, "Sir, may I speak to this sailor?"

The Captain gave his permission, "Very well."

The sailor looked at Seaman Takemura and said, "It's been a long time since I've seen you Seaman, but aren't you Seaman Takemura who serves under the command of the famous Captain Sakuragi?"

Seaman Takemura is well known among the sailors of

the Imperial Navy as a man who is cheerful, skilled in artillery, and in possession of unbelievable strength in his arms. A face very familiar to the sailors was unexpectedly before them on this ship of the Imperial Navy far from the shores of home.

The surprised Seaman stared and tapped his head as he said, "Oh! I certainly am Takemura Shinpachiro serving under Captain Sakuragi. I'm sorry, but I've completely forgotten who you are. Who are you?"

"I am the signal man who previously served under Captain Takao and is now serving under Captain Matsushima, the captain of the *Sunrise*. The *Sunrise* is a ship that was built at a shipyard at the mouth of the Thames River in England. Under Captain Matsushima's command, she left the Gulf of Aden early yesterday morning and was cruising through the Indian Ocean when your balloon fell from the sky and we rushed to help you. What a strange connection?" he stopped speaking and took a step back.

Those words! If a thoughtless man had heard them, probably nothing would have happened. But without thinking, Seaman Takemura and I looked at each other smiling. We didn't know whether we had been flying above the Atlantic Ocean or the Arabian Sea as we had suspected on the balloon. Our first joy was the words spoken by the sailor. It's just as I thought, this was the Indian Ocean, not far from Colombo where we were headed and Kanran Island where we will meet Captain Sakuragi again.

I slapped my knee when I heard that name Captain Matsushima.

Dear Reader, Do you know who Captain Matsushima is? I had never met the Captain, but having heard what good friends he and Captain Sakuragi were, I could never forget him. I remembered that he is the elder brother of Harue, Hideo's uncle. Four years ago, Harue, the wife of my close friend Hamajima Takebumi left her husband to be by her brother, Captain Matsushima, as he lay in his sickbed in Japan. With her cherished son Hideo, she left the Port of Naples in Italy on the same steamship as I. But on the way home to far off Japan, we were attacked by a terrifying pirate ship in the middle of the black Indian Ocean. I still didn't know whether she survived the sinking of the ill-fated *Crescent Moon*.

The Captain had been awaiting orders due to his illness when he heard. His health was restored and he was now navigating the military cruiser *Sunrise*. That explains why I wondered who he looked like when I saw him earlier. The Captain of the *Sunrise* is Captain Matsushima, Harue's older brother and Hideo's uncle. When I looked up and saw Captain Matsushima's face, he was scrutinizing Seaman Takemura's face and my face, and for a moment exchanged glances with Lieutenant Whiskers and began to quietly ask a question. The Captain said to me, "From conversations between the sailor of this ship and your companion Seaman Takemura, I believe you are connected to a Captain Sakuragi Shigeo, a close friend of mine. Is that so?"

He resumed staring at me as I nodded, and continued, "In fact, when I heard that you two had mysteriously dropped from the sky with a large balloon, I imagined something in my heart. There is nothing like imagination. If you are connected to our Sakuragi, this mysterious event may have some connection to the fate of Captain Sakuragi. I know a great deal about his aspirations. I am aware that he has hidden away on an unknown desert island in the Indian Ocean with close to forty sailors.

"Five years ago, when he informed me that he would

be absent from the naval port at Yokosuka for a long time, he said with determination, 'Five years from now, we will have achieved a great success, then I will see you again.' Five years have passed, but I've heard no news about him. All that time, I have prayed for his health each day and for the success of his great work. Well, Sakuragi has probably achieved this great goal and completed the major military weapon he had agonized over."

In a lowered voice, he said, "But when I saw this balloon unexpectedly over the Indian Ocean, particularly one carrying Seaman Takemura, who is said to be the right-hand man of Captain Sakuragi, I thought something out of the ordinary had happened to Sakuragi on that desert island. As a consequence, you two were entrusted with a critical mission, said farewell, and took to the sky."

"You're right! It's just as you say," I said as I stepped forward.

Seaman Takemura was so moved he said, "Captain, Captain Sakuragi has a big problem."

Together we summarized Captain Sakuragi's Undersea Warship, the circumstances of the success, midnight on February 21, and the events from the terrible tsunami caused by a landslide just before leaving Asahi Island on the verge of the Captain's success, the destruction of the warehouse in the Secret Shipyard, the loss of the twelve barrels, and our assignment to this mission. We ended with a request, "Captain, we must urgently proceed to the port in Colombo, India, obtain the twelve secret chemicals, and arrive at Kanran Island to rendezvous with *Lightning* by dawn on the twenty-fifth."

The listening sailors looked at each other amazed. The bold Lieutenant Whiskers cried out in surprise as he sprung from his seat and looked at Captain Matsushima.

In his fervor, the Captain looked up unaware of his crushing grip on the handle of his saber.

"Sakuragi's Undersea Warship is finished?" he asked then fell silent for a moment. With arms folded, he looked to the eastern sky.

"Since Sakuragi's party has experienced an unforeseen calamity, by dawn of the twenty-fifth, he will be waiting for your support near Kanran Island? Very well, with our help, he will have no reason for concern. For the Empire of Japan, for the Imperial Navy, and for Captain Sakuragi's honor, we shall exert our full effort in support of *Lightning*."

He stood, spread a nautical chart on the table beside him, and began making detailed measurements of the latitude.

"The most suitable as well as the closest trading port from here is the Port of Colombo. By sea, it is approximately 2,860 miles away. Kanran Island is slightly less than 3,635 miles from there. If we drop anchor in Colombo three nights from now, obtain the twelve secret chemicals needed by *Lightning*, and immediately send a coded telegram to receive permission from the government, then at full speed we will be able to reach Kanran Island in time!"

He looked at Lieutenant Whiskers beside him, "Lieutenant Todoroki! Full speed ahead to the Port of Colombo. Starboard signal on."

Lieutenant Whiskers' actual name is Lieutenant Todoroki.

"Yes sir," he replied and ran out to the foredeck.

Captain Matsushima returned to the map. Just then, from the waist deck came the six bells signaling eleven o'clock in the morning. Clang! Clang! Clang! Clang! Clang! Clang!

Seaman Takemura and I felt as though a heavy load

had been lifted from our shoulders. We were elated. At this joyous moment, we were finished recounting our mission, but I had many questions I wished to ask Captain Matsushima and information I wished to relate. The safety of his sister Harue, news about her husband Hamajima Takebumi, and things I didn't speak of earlier—I actually thought he would die of shock—like news about the last three years spent on Asahi Island with his nephew Hideo who was alive and well.

I attempted to speak several times, but the Captain's single-minded focus on the map stopped me. He was absorbed with studying the terrain and the depth of the ocean near Kanran Island in order to rendezvous with the Undersea Warship. The cabin was hushed. Outside were the sounds of the waves breaking on the sides of the ship, the wind passing the masthead, and the commands of officers echoing on the bridge.

Without thinking, I left my seat to watch the activities of the officers and sailors on the top, at the barbette, and at the battle turret on deck. What I saw startled me, as if shocked by electricity. From the hatchway on the afterdeck appeared two people walking toward me while chatting with a lively group of young officers wearing epaulets. The two were wearing civilian clothes on this military vessel. One was a portly gentleman with a commanding presence and the other, a beautiful woman, reminiscent of an angel! They were Hamajima Takebumi from whom I had parted four years earlier and his wife Harue, Captain Matsushima's sister and Hideo's mother, who I thought had departed this world.

I rubbed my eyes hard. Yes, it was them! Wild with joy, I twisted Seaman Takemura's head around so he could see them.

"Seaman! Look over there! There's Hamajima! And Harue!" I shouted.

The startled Seaman stretched on his toes to look, "Wh...Wh...Where? Who?"

At the table beside us, Captain Matsushima noticed the commotion and looked at us a bit concerned.

"This is strange. Who are you? Do you know Hamajima Takebumi and Harue?"

I leaned forward and said, "I am Yanagawa who was separated from Harue when the *Crescent Moon* sank four years ago."

Captain Matsushima flushed slightly and as he asked, "So do you know...do you have any idea what happened to my young nephew Hideo?" my eyes quickly moved to the Hamajimas just as they caught sight of me.

"Ah!" slipped from Harue's lips, then she looked back at her husband.

I went toward them, and they came toward me. I thought my legs were going to give out!

27

THE CAPTAIN'S CABIN

The sun was high in the sky. The flags of the Imperial Navy danced in the cool winds on the gaff of the warship *Sunrise*. Krupp guns, Gatling guns, 47-mm anti-tank guns, and portholes arranged near the bulwark were pointed at the far-off sky. We listened to the sounds of waves breaking nearby as we sat on the sofa in the Captain's cabin, once again face to face after such a long time.

Without saying a word, Hamajima Takebumi grabbed my hand. Harue turned to me and said, "Mr. Yanagawa, I never thought I would see you..."

Seaman Takemura stood beside me totally clueless.

As if spurred by Harue's words, Captain Matsushima asked me, "Is...is Hideo alive?"

I cheerfully yelled, "Oh yes, Captain Matsushima, Takebumi, Harue! Happily, Hideo is alive. He's safe."

Captain Matsushima and Takebumi beamed as they talked to each other and twisted their mustaches. Just like a woman, Harue dabbed at the tears she was unable to stop with her red silk handkerchief and said, "Is this a dream? If it isn't, I am so very happy."

"Nope, it's not a dream," chimed in the unpolished Seaman, then shouted, "Ma'am! You say it is a dream. Well, right now, that cute Hideo is alive and well on Asahi Island with our esteemed Captain Sakuragi. Sometimes he'll look to the distant sky of Japan from the cliff on the shore with the sailors and his pet Lightning and look forward to leaving that desert island and being with you again one day sooner."

"And you are?" the couple asked as they turned to Seaman Takemura.

I introduced him, "This is Seaman Takemura. During our three years on the desert island, he has become Hideo's best friend."

Seaman Takemura and I took turns recounting the story: our drifting to Asahi Island, the extraordinary Undersea Warship, life on the island, how much Hideo has grown since being torn from his mother's arms more than four years ago, the kind nurturing education from the wise and courageous Captain Sakuragi to become a navy man as his father had wished, and watching him become wiser and braver with each passing day. If fortune is on the side of Captain Matsushima and the Hamajimas, they only need to wait to be happily reunited with him not far from here. When we finished, all three were both astonished and euphoric. The Captain never stopped twisting his mustache. The formidable Hamajima said with confidence, "I couldn't be happier. The sinking of the *Crescent Moon* may have been good fortune for Hideo. Now, he is no longer hidden from this world. For him to grow up while receiving the fine education kindly provided by Captain Sakuragi, I believe is far better than graduating from the world's premiere school."

In a voice unable to contain her joy, Harue said, "How could I thank everyone for taking such good care of my child? I don't have words to express my gratitude."

The dimples on her cheeks filled with tears.

"Yeah, well, the fellow is this tall." The Seaman sprang up, "He's gotten big. When you meet him at Kanran Island, you won't believe it."

"Oh."

In a more serious tone, he added, "We haven't told you what else he does. He hunts lions and sumo wrestles. He can even beat some of the weaker sailors."

"On the other hand, he's pretty much turned black."

"Oh my," Harue giggled, covering her mouth, "So he has become black..."

"Like a period," the jesting Seaman answered. As the Captain, Hamajima, and I burst out laughing, Harue's enchanting eyes looked longingly at the faraway water and sky to the south.

I leaned forward and said, "We've only told our story. Now it's your turn," and looked at Harue.

"Harue, just like you, I also thought I would never see you again in this world. This is truly remarkable. How did you survive the sinking?"

I continued, "If I remember correctly, four years ago, I was holding Hideo when the *Crescent Moon* sank and we plunged into the sea. I called your name a few times, but heard only the wind and the waves. No. One time I thought I heard a reply, but was confused. Later, we drifted onto Asahi Island. When I told this story to Captain Sakuragi, he predicted your fate, and had no doubt that you were alive. But Hideo and I had given up hope of seeing you again in this world."

Harue recalled the frightful scene that night four years ago.

"Oh, that was truly an awful time. The sounds were deafening as the *Crescent Moon* sank. I fell several dozen feet down into the turbulent waves. I heard you calling my name when I resurfaced. I called out twice, but surrounded by darkness, I couldn't tell where I was, so we ended up separated for such a long time.

"Fortunately, I clung to the buoy you had given me. The next morning while floating between the waves, I saw a ship that resembled the pirate ship at a distance repeatedly submerging diving equipment. As I watched, a passing mail boat from England rescued me. We turned around and about a month later I was back home again in Naples.

"When I returned home to my husband and could only cry, there were many rumors about the sinking of the *Crescent Moon*. I felt abandoned by fate and simply grieved. I heard many rumors and soon believed both you and Hideo had died. I was also worried about my sick brother in Japan. Fortunately, he eventually recovered, which I received word about while on the mail boat. I was relieved, but abandoned thoughts of returning to Japan.

"That was four years ago. With this chance meeting, I have so much I want to talk to you about. As if in a dream, I feel as happy as seeing the sun after a long rain and can do nothing but thank heaven. Yes, my brother was fully recovered about three months after I returned to Naples and is now healthy. As you can see, he is now commanding this new ship *Sunrise*, constructed in England."

When she finished, she smiled at her brother and her husband.

28

THE MEMORIAL WARSHIP

Captain Matsushima listened to our interesting conversation as he continuously twisted his mustache.

Hamajima Takebumi spoke next.

"Harue is a bit of a complainer. But that's how women are. Ha ha ha. I was stunned when I heard that the *Crescent Moon* had sunk. Only Harue safely returned, and your whereabouts were unknown. When I was resigned to the drowning in the Indian Ocean of you and Hideo, who I had hoped would grow into a capable man in the Imperial Navy and contribute to the country, rather than cry, I felt a bitter pain."

Instantly, he was laughing loudly.

"Well, even I complained. No, I didn't complain, I was discouraged. Around that time, many European newspapers had written detailed accounts of the *Crescent Moon* disaster and savaged the cowardly behavior of the captain, the crew, and the others. There was also a story entitled *The Spirit of the Japanese People* that praised your behavior. But I couldn't bear the heartbreak. I asked myself how could the captain and the rest of those cowards behave in such a manner. Well, he did return unharmed to his country, but sanctions from the law and society took care of him. He was handed a severe punishment and met many bitter experiences, then disappeared to parts unknown."

"Serves him right! That's great!" blurted out Seaman Takemura.

Smiling, I placed my hand on my heart and asked, "Takebumi, did you and your wife continue to live near the Port of Naples? Why are you on this warship returning to Japan?

"My imagination may be a little overactive, but there's something I have been pondering for a while. Is there some connection between your dear son's name, Hideo (日出雄) and the naming this new cruiser Sunrise (日の出)?"

"It would probably be better if you talked to Whiskers about this?"

Just then, the always easygoing Lieutenant Whiskers—actual name, Lieutenant Todoroki—rushed into the room. He went directly to Captain Matsushima and said a few words. After finishing his report, he turned to me and cheerfully said, "Sir! You may say that naming this cruiser *Sunrise* is a memorial to Hideo as you imagined. You may see it that way. As you know, Mr. Hamajima intended to educate Hideo to become a capable navy man and defend the Empire of Japan. However, he believed that all his hopes had turned into foam on the sea with the sinking of the *Crescent Moon*.

"Unable to offer his son to the nation, he would sponsor a warship and accomplish his long-held wish. Spending half of his fortune, the warship *Sunrise* was built at the Thames Shipyard in England over the last three years. This warship is the latest Third Class cruiser. It has a displacement of 2,800 tons, a speed of 23 knots, and resembles the Imperial Warship *Akashi*, but is faster, has 20-mm defense armor in flat parts and 53-mm on inclines. The gun ports were equipped with two 8-inch mortar guns, six 12-cm mortar guns, twelve 47-mm mortar guns, and four machine guns.

"The Japanese government gladly followed Mr. Hamajima's wishes. A special investigation was conducted in the Ministry of the Navy, and Captain Matsushima was promptly appointed to head the committee responsible for bringing the ship to Japan. Now, as the Captain of this vessel, he is taking the ship to Japan. More than as an escape from the weariness of foreign skies, Mr. and Mrs. Hamajima boarded this ship at the Port of Naples, and are returning to the Japan of beautiful mountains and clear waters to formally deliver the ship as its sponsors," explained Lieutenant Todoroki while twisting his mustache in reverse.

"The warship *Sunrise*! I believe that this name clearly resembles Hideo. However, Mr. Hamajima is definitely not a publicity hound. He did not request this name. Everything was decided by the government of Japan. The result of a solemn process was to name the warship using the three characters of Hi-No-De. However, I do not believe that the similarity between the names was a coincidence."

I couldn't keep from shouting, "I doubt it's a coincidence."

Seaman Takemura wiped his brow and laughingly offered, "Wow, the reasons for congratulations are piling up. A new warship is donated. The Undersea Warship will appear. The Imperial Navy of Japan is prospering."

Captain Matsushima also smiled.

"Indeed, as the seaman said, the Japanese Navy deserves congratulations. Before long, we will meet Captain Sakuragi near Kanran Island. The warship

Sunrise and Captain Sakuragi's *Lightning* will line up stem to stern and, with the flags of the Imperial Navy rustling high in the sea breeze, arrive at the Imperial Navy Port. It will be a heroic and a joyous time."

Lieutenant Todoroki raised both hands and shouted with delight. Hamajima Takebumi was impatient to speak, "The truth is all human affairs are left to Providence. I don't know whether our wanderings will be fortunate. Today, I am thankful not only for the warship *Sunrise*, but to be able to offer Hideo, who we had once mourned, to the nation." Flush with satisfaction, he turned to his wife.

I, too, deeply felt that all human affairs are left to Providence. This thought jogged my memory. The unforgettable incident from over four years ago occurred when Harue, Hideo, and I left the pier at the Port of Naples. Annie, the elderly Italian woman who was Hideo's nanny, repeatedly talked about the Day of the Devil, the Devil's Hour, and the curse of gold and pearls in order to stop us from leaving that night. Naturally, at that time, I laughed at her insane ramblings and found them ridiculous. However, thinking about it now, it may have been chance, but there were similarities to the omens of various past disasters. I once brought this up with Captain Sakuragi while on Asahi Island, the sensible Captain was skeptical, but I couldn't eliminate all doubt from my heart. This was my opportunity to ask Harue if she knew anything more.

29

SATSUMA BIWA

Raising her eyebrows, Harue said, "Oh yes, that! You have a fine memory. Annie did not have that strange affair in mind, but it did occur to her later. Everything I'm going to tell you is the truth. Here is what happened."

As the gentle sea breeze swept back the hair on her temples, she began, "Annie never stopped talking about the Day of the Devil and the Devil's Hour. The *Crescent Moon* left port that night and, as she predicted, mysteriously sank in the Indian Ocean. When I was rescued by the English mail boat and returned to my home in Naples, Annie had already vanished. I searched for her, but no one knew where she went. I found this quite strange. Then one day, I received a letter from a cloistered convent in a desolate village in Mt. Urbino far from Naples. The letter was without a doubt in Annie's handwriting. That letter filled in the details."

"Wh...Wh...What did it say?" Seaman Takemura and I jumped up.

Her bright eyes clouded.

"It's so sad. According to the letter, Annie heard about the sinking of the *Crescent Moon* and became a nun as an apology to us. This circumstance is a tragedy.

"Annie's only son is quite a scoundrel. He left home a dozen or so years ago and disappeared. She always used to say, 'My son never listened to me. Soon after he left home on that cursed day in October, he was taken by a sea snake.' I found it strange for him to have been taken by a sea snake. Italians tend to use colorful turns of phrase like that in everyday speech, but I finally understood this one from the letter.

"Her son being captured by a sea snake was not reality. In fact, he seemed to have met with the crew members of a notorious pirate ship, a demon of the Indian Ocean, drank blood and became a sailor on a pirate ship named *Sea Snake*. Thus, Annie was left alone at home and eventually became a member of our household staff. As you know, she is a principled woman. This event occurred exactly two nights before we left the Port of Naples while she was still in our service.

"Annie had gone out on an errand and chanced upon her son near the seawall. No matter how evil a person, the love between a mother and a child is unique. 'Come with me,' she said. The upright Annie took her son to a small restaurant nearby. From the paltry sum in her purse, she treated her son to his favorite dishes. As tears streamed down her face, she scolded him, 'Well, son, what are you doing these days? Of course, you haven't reformed your ways? Have you?'

"Her indifferent son slurred, 'Not again. Ma, you're too damn good. Does being a goody two-shoes work in this world?' and took a gulp of liquor. 'I got a big job coming up. That's why I'm here at this port. We're gonna leave two nights from now. If we succeed, I'll pass on a measly hundred or two to you. Shhhh! This is our secret.'

"He had said too much.

"Annie was stunned. The rumor was that the *Crescent Moon* loaded with unheard of mountains of gold and pearls would leave the Port of Naples and head to the East. The *Sea Snake*, a threat to all, was furtively anchored beside it. However, when she asked around, no one knew a thing. How surprised Annie must have been when she realized, although uncertain, that her son was at that port with pirates.

"She did not say that the *Crescent Moon* with us on board was the target of the *Sea Snake* that would leave the Port of Naples at the same time on the same day. When she realized that the big job her son spoke of was an attack on the *Crescent Moon* to steal its treasure, she seemed to condemn the evil deed, but never tried to dissuade him.

"Her cutthroat son guessed that she knew and said, 'Well Ma, seems you figured it out. I'm done for. You know if anyone finds out about this plan, my head will fly. If it leaks, things will get bad. You don't have the option of choosing your master's house. Fires happen and you don't live alone.'

"Like the devil, he threatened her.

"Annie had a heart and was heartless. Although she quickly rushed back to our home, she couldn't do anything. Not only worried about her son being killed, she believed that she had brought a frightening vendetta down on our home. In the end, her heart was shattered. She was committed to that strange affair. Her plan was to keep us from boarding the *Crescent Moon*. Unfortunately, not a soul believed her.

"The ship departed on Devil's Hour on the Day of the Devil. We dismissed Annie's peculiar behavior and sailed off into disaster. When Annie heard the news of the sinking of the *Crescent Moon*, she no longer lived in this world. She had hidden away in a convent far from this world as a sincere apology to us and to pray for her son to repent. Annie probably went to a world free from sin and impurity in a hermitage on the grass of Mt. Urbino. The piracy of that cruel son is an atrocity on the waves of the Indian Ocean."

When she finished, Harue turned her eyes to the sky. Surprising myself, I slapped my knee. The short-tempered Seaman Takemura scanned the vast sea restless to take action.

"This place, the Indian Ocean. That insolent punk is somewhere out there," he said and eyed the machine guns on board.

"This is a wonderful time. My greatest wish is to slaughter those pirates who were so cruel to you."

"Yes! Excellent!" shouted Lieutenant Todoroki, clapping wildly. Captain Matsushima, Takebumi, and two or three seated sailors smiled at his brave face and exchanged glances. The *Sunrise* seemed to be tossing blossoms of the tide to the port and starboard as it slashed through the waves.

I don't have words to describe the warm reception Seaman Takemura and I received on the ship. The ship kicked up billowy waves as it headed to the Port of Colombo. However, there wasn't enough time for me to tell the entire tale, which resembled a novel, unbroken like the waves on the Indian Ocean to the Captain, Takebumi, Harue, Lieutenant Todoroki, and the other officers and sailors gathered on the deck. Buffeted by a crisp breeze under the soothing sun, I traced back to the events of the sinking of the *Crescent Moon*. The hardships we faced as we drifted in the small boat. The sudden shower. The unusual tale of catching the shark. Hideo holding his nose to beat back the stench of the rotting shark flesh. Later drifting onto Asahi Island. The delicious coconut fruit. The gorilla attack. The sudden appearance of Captain Sakuragi. The strange echoes of iron and the sheer cliff. The unique fierce dog, Lightning. The interesting daily lives of the Captain, Hideo, and the thirty plus sailors who awoke to starlight each morning and walked home under moonlight each evening. Moments of leisure filled with happy chats over tea, amusing boat races, and baseball games.

They smiled and laughed and seemed to enjoy the stories. I also shared details about erecting the monument on Asahi Island. The singular automatic adventure car. The action scenes as we dashed deep into the mountains and the marshes. The great struggle with the savage animals and snakes. The danger to Seaman Takemura's leg. The fall into the quicksand sinkhole due to our curiosity and our narrow escape. The separation of Hideo from Lightning. The giant balloon descending toward us from the mountain denuded of trees. The festive scene on Empire Day.

Then I told the strange tale beginning with the disaster on the night of *Lightning*'s test run until our current mission. They were captivated by our adventure. As I described our life on the desert island, the source of many jokes and blunders, who stood beside me, Seaman Takemura, enthusiastically chimed in. Slapping the backs and clapping the hands of *Sunrise*'s sailors from time to time, he had become a favorite on the ship. Like me, Seaman Takemura was an honored guest on this warship, but he was also a sailor, a member of the warship family, with a winning personality among the sailors and adept in artillery and navigation. He never had time for reflection since boarding this warship.

Starting with Captain Matsushima, the entire crew of

the warship *Sunrise* swore to exhaust all their energies for the sake of the venerated Captain Sakuragi. In contrast, I often fretted over my desire to work like the sailors on this warship at least as a small payment for the happiness and gratitude I felt in my heart. However, military discipline on a warship is strict and cannot be altered. A man who is not an active military man on a ship cannot climb up to the mizzen top, cannot work in the machine room, cannot do a thing. So I would sit and look around, stand and look around, gaze at the endless ocean waves from the bow, watch the flags of the Imperial Navy flying on the gaff near the bulwark flap in the wind, and peek at the machine guns. The tedium was unbearable, I ached to take action.

Soon evening fell, the most enjoyable time for the crew of a warship out at sea. Most of the off-duty officers and sailors gathered at the aft deck under the big sky to sing songs and sword dance with abandon. Seaman Takemura frequently joined his comrades in the revelry. At that moment, I thought I heard a slight disturbance coming from somewhere. The whiskers of Lieutenant Todoroki rushed forward and spoke to the Seaman who was standing beside me, "Hey, Seaman Takemura, I heard you're pretty good at playing the Satsuma biwa. Why don't you play us a song?," then ordered him to go get his treasured biwa. Near the 15-cm machine guns and below the aft side of the bridge, young officers and old seadogs said, "This oughta be interesting," and strained to hear. The Seaman sat cross legged beneath the fluttering flags at the stern of the Imperial Warship and sang out as he strummed and struck the biwa.

> Towering mountains in the clouds.
> There to climb, but never to cross.
> The sky dips into the sea.

If there to cross, it must be crossed.
Our Akitsushima, a dazzling red.
An island far off in the eastern sea.
In the middle of the sea.
Like a ship afloat...

The high-pitched melody soared like a fierce eagle beating the wind. And like the cry of valley water dammed by rocks, the low-pitched melody harmonized with the sounds of the winds over the Indian Ocean pierced by the masthead and the waves breaking against the ship. For a moment, the sounds echoed throughout the ship. When the performance ended, Lieutenant Whiskers was the first to leap up applauding.

"Marvelous. A true artist. Don't discount this man!"

"Seaman, now, how about an arm wrestling match to see who's the best...," he said and thrust out his iron-like arm. Lieutenant Whiskers was a famous arm wrestler. However, Seaman Takemura knew little of this and had confidence in his superior strength.

"Okay, I'm ready," he said, set aside his biwa and began combat. One twist and down. The match was over.

"Hmm, I'm a weakling," the Lieutenant roared with laughter, "What...What happened? I didn't defeat this Takemura. We'll see who's number one."

They fought again, and he lost again.

"This was not my intention."

He looked at his arm and rubbed it, but was defeated. As he looked around, the officers and sailors of the *Sunrise* were chuckling. Hamajima Takebumi was laughing boisterously. Harue was hiding her smile behind a handkerchief.

"Well, too bad," Seaman Takemura said and thrust out

his hairy shins, "Lieutenant, let's see who's the best leg wrestler."

"Leg wrestling?" asked Lieutenant Todoroki frowning. However, the Lieutenant did not like to lose and stuck out his legs. After one push, he cried out, "Ouch! Oouuu...ch...ch...ch," and sprang back.

"That hurt. It felt like Takemura had hidden kitchen knives in his legs."

"Is he that strong?"

A mob of officers and sailors gathered to challenge him. Of course, Takemura's legs rippled with muscles. Everyone was forced down in one thrust and drew back in pain. Seaman Takemura's color changed slightly, and he wriggled his nose. A hero was on the deck of the warship *Sunrise.*

"Takemura, excuse me for saying, but you have defeated every man on the *Sunrise.* Well, now it's my turn."

From the shadows of the large mast emerged the black shape of a brawny young ensign. During his time at the Naval Academy, this man was the champion eater, had a lung capacity of 5,200, a grip strength of 78, and could pole vault 10 feet and run 600 yards in 86 seconds. In his third year, he was the best rower on the squad. His rowing power was said to be unrivaled.

"Okay, come on!"

His iron legs met Seaman Takemura's legs armed with kitchen knives. As they fought, they grunted, groaned, and both turned bright red. The deck pulsed with excitement.

"Enough already. Stop this. You'll break your legs," said Lieutenant Whiskers as he circled them. They ended in a draw.

Captain Matsushima peered down from the bridge, twisting his mustache and smiling.

30

A GREAT SEA BATTLE ON A
MOONLIT NIGHT

According to plan, the warship *Sunrise* arrived at
the Port of Colombo on the western shore of the
Indian continent two evenings later. Captain Matsushima,
Seaman Takemura, and I made our way through coconut
and banana groves concealing the shore, and climbed high
up near the seawall to streets lit by electric lights that
tricked you into believing it was day.

We secretly procured the chemicals for *Lightning*
entrusted to us by Captain Sakuragi and sealed them in
twelve barrels. With no need to hire a ship, we loaded the
barrels onto the *Sunrise*. Simultaneously, Captain
Matsushima received approval from the government by
encrypted telegram and ordered the ship to head to
Kanran Island to rendezvous with the Undersea Warship
at daybreak on the twenty-fifth.

Kanran Island was about 1,500 nautical miles from the
Port of Colombo. Before long, the two wise and courageous Captains, one on the deck of the new warship *Sunrise*
and the other on the deck of the new *Lightning*, would meet
across the waves at dawn on a clear calm day and look up

at the flags of the Imperial Navy. The two ships would line up in formation several thousand miles from shore. Imaginations would be stirred by the image of the morning scene of cotton roses. As night fell, Takebumi and Harue were chatting near the bridge, glanced by a gentle sea breeze. They had waited a long time to be reunited with their beloved son.

The voyage was uneventful for four days and nights. The sounds of the waves rebounded off the port and starboard. Each moment brought us closer to the finale. The profile of an island that appeared to be Kanran Island was identified in an area covered by clouds and smoke. The day was February 25. The time was between two and three on a gloomy morning. A vivid waning moon crossed the sky. Only the noise of the ship's steam engine could be heard above the lizard-like waves.

No one on the *Sunrise* could sleep. Beginning with Captain Matsushima on the bridge, a group of officers each gripping a pair of binoculars scanned the sea as the waves sprayed their epaulets sparkling in the moonlight. The sailors quietly talked and laughed in a few scattered groups on the deck. Seaman Takemura eyes widened, he fidgeted and said, "At last, we're close to Kanran Island. The Captain's Undersea Warship may already be in the lee of the island. Maybe he hasn't left Asahi Island yet. No, no, he's already there waiting."

Hamajima Takebumi was leaning against the huge gun at the stern and patting his fine beard. The smiling Harue, more beautiful than an angel, looked up as she walked to her husband. The clouds stopped in the sky and the birds singing above the waves seemed to be praising us. Those pleasant moments were broken by shouts coming from the gangway.

All sound on the ship was silenced. Almost three

nautical miles from the ship, north of what appeared to be Kanran Island, were two groups of islands resembling coiled venomous dragons. A point of light flashed on from the lee of the island. Then came another point and another until a total of seven mysterious ships had raised a round lantern high on its foremast. The ships formed into a long column and came toward us. Bathed in moonlight, the ship at point spewed black smoke. It had two funnels and two masts! Four years had passed, but I had not forgotten. When I shouted, "The *Sea Snake* is coming! That's the *Sea Snake*!" Captain Whiskers jumped up and ran to the battle turret.

Explosive signals streamed like glittering meteors from the bow of the *Sea Snake*. They were nighttime signals to warn other ships. The audacious pirate ship launched the signals to attract the attention of our Imperial Warship. As expected, all eyes were directed there.

Captain Whiskers, who had run toward the battle turret, returned near me and yelled, "Unidentified ship! Unidentified ship! That ship is trying to send us some sort of signal."

Assessing the situation and the seven ships, the *Sea Snake* was clearly trying to signal our ship for some reason. However, I was suspicious. On the seas in today's world, all nations share daytime signals, but nighttime signals are the secret signals of each nation's navy. Moreover, the world's nations do not share distress signals except for important or simple signals like the explosive signals launched by the *Sea Snake*.

If the mystery ship is testing those signals on us, what steps should we take. Looking at the *Sea Snake*, electric lights beamed on the top mast, lower mast, bow, stern, starboard, and port. Flooding the ship with light was just a trick. The strange shadow of one person appeared below the light and raised signal flags high on the mast beam. The mysterious but sophisticated ship would use daytime signals under the electric lights. Triangular and rectangular signal flags with various patterns blew in the wind. They signaled, "Halt warship! Halt warship!"

Captain Matsushima shouted an order and our entire ship flooded with electric light. The signalman first-class stood at the foot of the signal mast and raised the signal flags as ordered.

"Unidentified ship! Identify yourself!"

Their reply fluttered in the wind, "We are the famous pirate ships of the Indian Ocean. You have kept us waiting. We are here to steal your newly built warship. Promptly raise a white flag and surrender. Try to delay and our seven armored ships will attack and destroy you."

As we watched, the ships lined up port to starboard along the horizon. We could see weapons glimmering under the moonlight reflecting off the decks of the seven pirate ships. A flash of anger ran through the officers and sailors on our ship. Among them the young ensign quickly gripped the handle of his saber awaiting the Captain's orders. The sailors, unmatched in daring, near the gangway and the porthole were ready to fight. Takebumi laughed coldly, while Harue was silent.

Furious, Seaman Takemura said, "Fool Pirates! You'll pay for this!" and ran to the 8-inch mortar guns on the starboard side. But he stopped cold realizing that by strict military discipline, although he possessed remarkable skills, like the sacred Mount Taishan, he was not a crew member and could not operate artillery nor fire guns. He could only grind his teeth with regret.

"Ah, crap. At times like this, I envy the sailors of this ship," he shouted and shook his fists as he stood firm with feet apart at the bow of the ship. Lieutenant Todoroki, twisting his mustache in reverse, averted his eyes and waited for orders from the Captain as he held a 12-cm gun with his right hand. Captain Matsushima was agitated for a moment, but calmly gave the order to the signalman to raise the signal flags with his reply.

"Fools! Pirates! Can't you see the flags of the Japanese Imperial Navy on our gaff?"

Instantly, all of the electric lights on the *Sea Snake* went out. The seven pirate ships kicked up black raging waves in a headlong rush toward us. One deafening shell shrieked past as it grazed our foremast. The Captain unsheathed his sword and stood tall on the control tower. He shouted an order. The war trumpet blared. The officers' epaulets glittered, the sailors took their positions. At that instant, shells from the pirate ships poured down like rain, no, like hail. We responded with machine guns firing 8-inch shells. The moon faded as artillery fire flew over the moonlit sea and a dim powdery smoke rose, a scene reminiscent of the night-time battle fought long ago in the Gulf of Taranto. Needless to say, the officers and sailors acted with courage. As civilians idly standing by, Takebumi and I stripped off our heavy coats and rushed to carry shells and gunpowder.

Seaman Takemura whipped around a large saber, ready for pirates to fly onto the deck if the pirate ships got close. Like a lone cherry blossom dancing in the air after a thunderstorm, Harue nursed the wounded sailors. I could see the fresh blood of the sailors of the Imperial Navy gushing onto her snow-white arms as she gently held them.

The sea battle began at two thirty in the morning and was still raging at daybreak. Our side, a loyal and courageous Imperial Warship. The enemy, pirates of the Indian Ocean, notorious throughout the world. The pirate ships had been waiting impatiently for this artillery battle. Three or four of the ships with their bows aligned hurtled toward us. The pirates readied themselves on deck to ram and swarm our ship. Posers! Our ship was roused to stain the sacred deck with the vile blood of the pirates.

Smoke from gunpowder cloaked the dark sea. Claps of thunder enveloped us. Captain Matsushima's order was clearly visible high above the control tower. His miraculous skill at the helm freed the 2,800-ton cruiser to maneuver unhindered. If the pirate ships attacked from the right, the starboard-side machine guns would assault them. If they came at us from the left, the port-side machine guns would fire.

The enemy was strong in giving chase and attacking. The seven armored ships approached again. The waves raged, and bitter winds blew wildly. The flags of the pirates were stained with blood. Who knew when the battle would end? Look! Far off on the sea, a spray plumed and the waves swelled. A lone torpedo boat bolted toward us. As the boat neared, I could make out the flags of the Imperial Navy flapping at the stern in the morning breeze! As I looked, I ran from the port to the starboard side.

Cries of "The Captain's here! The Captain's here! Captain Sakuragi's *Lightning* is coming," reverberated throughout the ship between gun blasts. The officers and sailors on the *Sunrise* trembled with excitement. Seaman Takemura standing at the bow had been slightly wounded on his right temple. With his bare hands, he wiped away the blood flowing into his eyes and looked out to the sea. The Undersea Warship swiftly closed in and overtook our ship. When about one thousand meters ahead of us, the Undersea Warship dove between the waves. In no time, a boom shook the air above the sea. As we watched, the bottom of one pirate ship was pulverized. Seawater sprayed as the ship sunk into the abyss. Then came another disturbance, and the bow of another ship was pointing up as the ship sank. The pirate flag stamped by the devil hit the waves three times, before disappearing before our eyes.

"That's Captain Sakuragi! Assist *Lightning*! Don't give those sailors reason to mock us. Attack!"

Without taking a breath, the brave crew of the *Sunrise* fired shells that ripped into the floundering pirate boats, already confused and scattering like marbles. One ship sunk immediately. Lieutenant Todoroki executed a successful simultaneous firing of torpedoes from the 12-cm guns.

In one last desperate act, one ship aimed at and rushed our ship only to be hit in the artillery storage. Fires blazed inside and outside the ship. The helm exploded, and the ship spun like a top. Unseen below the waves, the Undersea Warship had smashed the enemy ship to pieces with its rotating ram with the force of a flash of lightning, like lightning slashing the spring wind. White dragons danced in the sky where the new fish-shaped torpedoes glided. Soon three pirate ships remained. As we watched, one ship listed from starboard to port and another from port to starboard while waves shot up. An avalanche of frantic pirates tumbled into the sea along with their large and small guns. Now only one pirate ship remained! It was the ship with two funnels and two masts, the *Sea Snake*!

The *Sea Snake* soon understood its predicament, furled its flag and tried to flee toward Kanran Island under cover of the black smoke. The Undersea Warship, no longer submerged, took chase on the waves like a dragon come to life. Our ship was silent for ten...twenty seconds, then came the echoes of thunder claps as the pointed ram pierced the starboard side of the pirate ship. The heinous *Sea Snake* plunged to the sea bottom, leaving only mist behind.

Night was over and the fiery sun rose in the lapis blue

sky in the east. A smile filled Captain Matsushima's face as he wiped away a cascade of sweat. As he looked around, he welcomed the sounds of *Kimigayo* sung by the brave officers and sailors of the warship *Sunrise* rising from the gangway, the mast top, and the battle turret above the dancing waves of the Indian Ocean. The flags flapped in the wind as cheers filled the air.

Both courage and joy were present. Takebumi and Harue's happiness left them speechless. Lieutenant Whiskers and Seaman Takemura wore a white band over minor wounds, one on the left side and the other on the right. As I jumped for joy, I gazed at the sunrise over the Indian Ocean. A crisp blast of wind skimmed the waves.

Lightning, destroyer of the *Sea Snake*, slowly circled the ship's bow and approached. I looked at the renowned lookout tower, on top were more than thirty sturdy sailors in black. Behind them stood the awe-inspiring Captain Sakuragi shading his eyes with both hands to see the deck of the warship *Sunrise*.

Near him stood Hideo in his sailor's uniform. His left hand held Lightning's collar. His right hand waved the flag of the Imperial Navy. A grin crossed his face as he looked up at us.

Dear Reader,

The Imperial Warship *Sunrise* and *Lightning*, which made a sudden but welcome appearance, had destroyed seven pirate ships, notorious worldwide for their evil acts, on the surging waves of the Indian Ocean. Under low hanging white clouds, they headed home side by side.

The lengthy telegram of this news dispatched last

night in Singapore should have reached the Department of the Navy in Japan by now.

Last Friday, the two ships rounded Cape Comorin on the Indian continent, passed the shores of Ceylon Island then the Bay of Bengal under the moon at dawn. They expressed gratitude for the salutes received from English, French, German, and Russian ships they encountered along the way.

The large and small Nicobar Islands and Salang Island were visible from the port and the starboard sides. The ships advanced through the dreamlike Strait of Malacca that forked to the west and to the east. They left trails of high surges and wild winds as they glided through the China Sea. These two ships may soon appear before your eyes.

I hope that even if you live in a secluded location in the mountains, you have already heard of these new and enjoyable events from special editions of the newspapers or from the rumor mill!

From the west near the Sea of Genkai, we will pass through the Strait of Bankan and enter the inland sea of Seto and exit through the Strait of Kii. We will turn at Shiozaki and pass through the Sea of Enshu, Suruga Bay, and proceed along the shores of Sagaminada.

Readers who live near the shore where the waves pound and ships turn should shade your eyes with your hands and look far out to sea from a second-floor window, a small hill near your home, or a cape on the shore. On the horizon where the sky meets the water, you may see curls of smoke, then a gleaming white cruiser will appear. Beyond that ship, you will see a seawater mist expelled by a mysterious ship, like a dragon or a whale.

Those with flags, wave your flags. Those with

daffodils, blow on your daffodils. Those with nothing, raise both hands and shout as loud as you can, *Banzai to the Empire!* and *Banzai to the Imperial Navy!* You will see the flags of the Imperial Navy flying from the gaff of the cruiser and at the stern of the mysterious ship above their decks as they gradually approach. At that time, yell out Banzai! three times to the warships *Sunrise* and *Lightning*. Captain Sakuragi, Seaman Takemura, Hideo, and the almost forty intrepid sailors will be standing at Lightning's lookout tower.

Captain Matsushima, Lieutenant "Whiskers" Todoroki, Takebumi and Harue Hamajima, and more than two hundred others will be on the deck of the *Sunrise*. Each will hold binoculars in their hands, wave handkerchiefs, and beam with joy in gratitude for your kindness. At that time, I will be at the stern of the warship *Sunrise*, beside the 8-inch anti-tank gun or near the gangway high above the sea, and respectfully hold my helmet high in my right hand. Together, we will give three cheers, "The Empire of Japan, *Banzai!* The Imperial Navy of Japan, *Banzai!*"

(From the deck of the warship *Sunrise*)

CREDITS

Japanese source text:

Aozora Bunko.
Oshikawa, Shunro. 海島冒険奇譚：海底軍艦 *(Kaitou Bouken Kitan: Kaitei Gunkan)*, Tokyo: Bunbudou, 1900.
Accessed December 11, 2014.
https://www.aozora.gr.jp/cards/000077/files/
1323_36134.html

Back cover photo:

National Diet Library Digital Collections.
Oshikawa, Shunro, 春浪快著集 *(Shunro Kaichoshu)*, Tokyo:
Okura Shoten, 1918.
Accessed September 11, 2016.
http://dl.ndl.go.jp/info:ndljp/pid/954295

www.jpopbooks.com

9 781734 964462